Of Sound Mind and Someone Else's Body

William Quincy Belle

Fate can be kind. Fate can be cruel. However, every once in a while, fate can be funny. This is the ~~lust~~ love story of how one man met the most unusual of women in the most unusual of circumstances.

BG Ltd.

Disclaimer
This is a work of fiction. Any names or characters, businesses or places, events or incidents, are fictitious. Any resemblance to actual persons, living or dead, is ... Well, what are the chances?

Chapter 1

Forty-eight hours. He was close. He was *so* close.

Alan stood at the balcony railing sipping a Scotch. He surveyed his domain: the buildings of New York City's core, the lit billboards, and the non-stop bustle of the street below. He was ready for the most important business deal of his career. If he pulled this off, he would cement his future as a major player in the company. He was going places; he could taste it.

Taking a deep breath, he let the vastness of the cityscape wash over him. Years of hard work and calculated moves had come to fruition, and he now lived in an eighth-floor condominium in an exclusive Upper East Side building with twenty-four-hour security, surrounded by designer furniture. He was on top of the world.

With a final gulp, Alan finished his drink and went inside, locking the sliding door. He sauntered across the open-plan living room to the kitchen and put his glass in the dishwasher.

After flicking off the light, he went to bed and gazed at the ceiling in the semi-darkness. As he mulled over his schedule for the next two days, he was more convinced than ever that he was on the verge of something extraordinary. Rolling onto his side, he drifted off to sleep.

***

Alan gagged. Something filled his mouth and throat. He couldn't breathe and thought he might throw up. Bringing both hands to his face, he fumbled around trying to free himself until his mouth became clear. He coughed violently as he gasped for air, then sat on his heels and braced his hands on his thighs. He shuddered.

"What's the matter?" The male voice sounded concerned. "Are you all right?"

Alan focused and realized he was staring at a man's legs with the trousers bunched below the knees. Confused, he looked up. There was the naked groin of a man sprouting an erect penis covered with a condom.

His eyes widened. *What the hell?*

He frantically scanned his surroundings. He was in a hotel room, neatly furnished as if it was one of the major chains. The man grinned at him. Alan gaped at the penis. Had that been in his mouth? A wave of nausea washed over him. This couldn't be real.

"Take a breath and let's try again." The man stepped forward and placed one hand on the back of Alan's head as he grasped the base of his penis with the other. He aimed his shaft and pulled.

Alan pushed the man's hips away. "Stop!" he cried out. But it wasn't his voice; it was a woman's.

The man leaned back. "I don't understand. You've always been able to take all of me with no difficulty. Throat problem?"

Alan blinked, dazed.

"Okay," the man said. "We can skip the deep throat. A normal blowjob will do just fine."

Confused, Alan regarded him and said, "I can't," again in a female voice.

"What?"

"I'm not doing that."

"Don't get me all worked up for nothing! I'll have blue balls for a week. I paid you the usual four hundred. Now, how about giving me a go?"

The man shifted forward again, holding out his erection. He grasped Alan's head and pulled it toward him.

"Jesus!" Alan muttered as he pushed against the man's hips. The two of them were at a stalemate. Horrified by the erection in front of his face, Alan slammed his fist into the man's scrotum. The man gasped and released his grip on Alan's head.

Alan scurried back as the man fell to his knees and flopped over into a fetal position, moaning. Staggering to his feet, Alan nearly fell too as one of his ankles buckled under him. He looked down and saw he was wearing high-heels and nylon stockings. He gawked for a moment then wobbled over to the wall mirror. His eyes widened and his jaw dropped. The face reflected back at him was not his: it was that of a woman.

He touched his face and saw in the mirror a slender hand touch the smooth skin of the woman's face. Unfamiliar blue eyes stared back at him. His mind reeled, unable to understand how this was possible. He had to be dreaming, but this didn't feel like a dream. Was he going to wake up at any moment?

He heard a groan behind him. The man on the floor mumbled, "Oh fuck," but didn't move.

Alan again gazed into the mirror. Leaning closer, he brushed aside shoulder-length blonde hair. He studied his features, focusing on the thick eye shadow and red lips. That was lipstick. He was wearing lipstick. Was he in drag? That wasn't his face, however. It wasn't his face at all.

He pulled on the blonde hair. It wasn't a wig. There was an odor. He held his hand up to his nose then grabbed some of his hair and inhaled. He was wearing perfume.

As he stood staring at himself, he glanced down at his chest. What were those? He ran his hands over the two protrusions. They were breasts. He had breasts.

An odd thought came to him. He reached down to his groin and passed a hand over the front of a short skirt. He couldn't feel a bulge. Lifting the hem of the skirt, he reached between his legs and felt around. No penis; no male genitalia. His face scrunched up in horror. *What the hell?*

He pulled up the skirt to expose a garter belt, stockings, and a pair of panties over top. He pulled the panties down and rubbed a hand between his legs.

"What the fuck's going on?" Alan muttered. He had a pussy. *He was a woman.*

Queasiness welled up in him and he felt light-headed. His stomach heaved, and he coughed up bile. The back of his throat burned. This couldn't be happening. He had to figure out what had taken place and how he could get out of this situation.

There was a purse on the table. He dumped out the

contents and sorted through them. The first thing he saw was a black rectangular box labeled *Stun Master*. There was a wallet, so he opened it and flipped through the cards until he found a driver's license. He looked at the photo and looked in the mirror. It was the same woman. The name given was Hana Toussaint with an address of 243 Charlton Street, Apartment 23.

His mind raced as he tried to make sense of this nightmarish situation. Who was this Hana Toussaint? What possible connection could there be between the two of them? How could he be in her body? How was it even possible to end up in someone else's body? If this wasn't a dream, it was something out of a science fiction movie.

He froze, wrinkling his forehead. Where was *his* body? If he had taken over the body of this Hana Toussaint, had somebody taken over *his*? Was it Hana? Had the two of them switched bodies?

He had to find himself. He had to find Alan Maitland and confront whoever was in that body. However, if he found Alan and Alan was still him, how would he ever sort out this craziness?

He shook his head. This was all too bizarre. There were so many questions, so many permutations of scenarios, that he couldn't make sense of anything. Nevertheless, he knew he had to find Alan.

He examined the address on the driver's license again. *Thank goodness.* It was in the same city. But he didn't understand where in the city he was, where this hotel was located. He found money inside the billfold and counted out four hundred and fifty-five dollars. *Of course.* The guy on the floor had said he'd paid four hundred bucks for a blowjob.

The door to the room opened with an explosive crash. A slim, tall man in a suit and tie ran in and stopped in the center of the room. "Don't you move!"

Alan whipped around to stare at this newcomer. The first man now sat in a chair. He still had one hand on his groin, but the other hand rested on a small table beside a cellphone. Alan hadn't been paying attention, too caught up in his own dilemma.

The slim man glanced at Alan. "Are you all right? What happened? What did he do?"

The seated man said, "What did *I* do? What did *she* do! Hell, Marvin, she punched me right in the nuts!" He shifted in his seat still holding his groin. "I was the one who called the answering service."

Marvin turned back to Alan astonished. "What's the matter with you? Mr. Smith is one of your regulars. Why in the hell would you do such a thing?"

Alan cowered against the wall. "Who are you?"

"Who am I? What's going on? Is this a joke?" The newcomer nodded to the man in the chair. "I apologize, Mr. Smith. I'm sure all of this is explainable. Let me get this straightened out." Then he walked up to Alan and spoke in a hushed tone. "What's gotten into you? Did he do something wrong? What's the problem?"

"I'm confused. I don't understand," Alan said, scrutinizing the room.

"What?" Marvin squinted. "Are you okay? Are you stoned or something?"

"I don't know."

Marvin took hold of his arm. "May I speak with you out in the hall?"

Alan wrenched his arm away. "What are you doing?"

"I think we need to have a little chat." Marvin said, his tone hushed but firm. He took Alan's arm again and tried to lead him to the door.

Alan jerked free of Marvin's grasp and scrambled for the taser. He pushed it against the tall man's midriff and pressed the button. There was a crackle of electricity as Marvin's body spasmed. Alan let go of the button, and Marvin collapsed in a heap.

He stood over the man wondering how long he would be incapacitated. He shot Mr. Smith a glance. Mr. Smith stared wide-eyed, his gaze shifting between Marvin and Alan.

With little thought, Alan went to the table and stuffed Hana's belongings back in the purse then rushed down the hall to the elevator. Twice he almost lost his balance. Frustrated, he muttered, "Christ, how do women walk in these things?"

Chapter 2

Alan stepped out of the hotel onto the still-busy street. The night air helped cool his flushed skin. He took a deep breath and looked around. It was in a nondescript middle-class city neighborhood made up of multi-story buildings with commercial fronts. He didn't recognize anything. *Where am I?*

He checked Hana's phone for GPS or a map, but the display showed *Enter your password.* He had to find somebody to give him directions.

He spotted the lit sign of a convenience store and headed down the street. In the light of the store window, he fished out the wallet and scanned the driver's license again.

A man walked by, and Alan called out, "Hey, buddy!"

The man continued until he looked at him and stopped dead. "Well, hey, baby. What are you doing out so late? As if I need to ask ..."

"Do you know where Charlton Street is?"

"If you invite me over, I may be able to help you." The man grinned.

Alan frowned. *What the hell had gotten into this guy?* "Charlton Street. Just tell me where Charlton Street is."

The man walked up and stood close. "Come on, sugar. How about being nice to a guy?" He reeked of booze.

"Oh, Christ," Alan said. He stomped into the store. Behind the counter, a teenage boy flipped through a magazine. "Do you know where Charlton Street is?" Alan asked.

The boy raised his head and stared, apparently mesmerized. Alan snapped his fingers in front of the boy's eyes. "Hey, you there. Where's Charlton Street?"

The boy stammered, "This is Varick. Go out the door, turn right, and go down five blocks." He stretched out his arm to point.

"Where's East Seventy-Eighth Street?"

"That's the Upper East Side. It's miles from here."

"Thanks."

Alan started for the door, then stopped and gaped at the

hand he had used to snap at the boy. He curled his fingers, then splayed them, looking at the long fingernails lacquered in bright red with little blue stars by the cuticles. He assumed the nails were fake, but they were so well done he couldn't tell. Then a surprising thought came to him: they were *his* fingernails.

He glanced up and saw a security mirror over the door. He could see that the teenage boy was leaning over the counter to stare at his backside. He looked down. The skirt he wore was short, so he showed a lot of leg. No wonder the boy was checking him out. Checking *him* out? *If only he knew the truth, he would run for the hills.* This was pushing cross-dressing to the limit.

Alan stepped out onto the sidewalk and paused before crossing the street. *Walking in heels is a bitch.* But he had no other shoes and no other choice. The thin stiletto forced him to pay extra attention to his balance by putting his foot down in the same manner with each step: in line, with short strides. Any variance of position meant the risk of stumbling. Alan had a newfound respect for women and the fine art of walking in heels. As a man he appreciated a well-turned ankle set off by a good shoe, but he had never considered what was involved in navigating terrain while being four or five inches off the ground. Who knew beauty could be so treacherous?

At each corner, he looked at the street sign to double-check the name and counted down the number of blocks while noting significant landmarks. With a block to go, he heard the boom of bass up ahead. A line had formed, and he figured it must be a late-night club. As he strode by, he realized people were staring at him, especially the men. It felt uncomfortable to be gawked at, and he wished they'd leave him alone.

At the end of the line stood a group of four young men. In the darkness, he couldn't tell, but he assumed they were around twenty. The club appeared to be of the type catering to those who wanted to belong to the latest scene. It promised flirtations with the opposite sex and a titillating tryst with a stranger. *Even though that's statistically improbable, these men came anyway*, Alan thought.

The four boys stopped talking among themselves and leered at him as he passed.

"Boy, would I love to fuck that," one of them commented.

Alan couldn't believe his ears. The utter gall of the boy! He stopped and doubled back. "Who said that?" Fury laced his voice.

None of the boys said a word.

"You're all going to this club with the hopes of getting laid, and the best line you have to get a woman is that you'd like to have sex? Fat chance you'll ever get lucky with a come-on like that."

Alan took a few steps away then stopped. "I'm sure some of the ladies in that club would love to get fucked tonight." He looked directly at the boy who had originally spoken. "Just not by you."

He continued down the sidewalk with a purposeful gait. *Piss off, you little shits.* He knew men could be morons — unsophisticated sex machines filled with so many hormones, it was surprising they didn't self-combust — but couldn't they have a little more savoir-faire regarding the ladies? No need to be crass!

Still seething, Alan almost missed the sign indicating that he had arrived at Charlton Street. Number two-forty-three turned out to be an older but well-maintained building with a stone staircase leading up to the main entrance. He fished around in the purse and found a ring of keys. It took three tries to get the right one.

He was relieved Hana lived on the second floor since he didn't think he could handle too many stairs. By stepping on each stair with just his toes, he avoided the problem of dealing with the actual heels. *It would probably be harder coming down*, he thought in dismay. First on the agenda when exploring Hana's apartment would be to find comfortable shoes.

Her apartment turned out to be a stylish one-bedroom. The main room contained a couch that sat before an entertainment center with bookshelves, a recessed kitchenette and a table with two chairs — all relatively new pieces. Several framed prints and decorative pieces adorned the walls.

Alan kicked off the shoes and let out a relieved sigh before exploring. Who was this woman, and what connection did she have to him? The bookshelf by the television held novels and textbooks. On the table, he found a text on human sexuality and, according to a notebook, indications that she was taking a course at Manhattan University. Mystified, he continued to the bedroom, which had a feminine look, with prints of Impressionist landscapes and a multicolored duvet with a floral motif.

From her extensive closet, he selected a comfortable outfit: jeans and a shirt. He wondered if he should call it a shirt or a blouse. *Are they the same thing?* He fumbled several times with the buttons and clasps — long fingernails were not conducive to manipulating small items. He looked at his hands with disbelief. *The things women have to put up with ...*

He was in the midst of removing his clothes when he caught his reflection in the full-length mirror on the closet door. He posed several ways, studying his form. *My form.* Well proportioned. Attractive. *My form.* He shook his head in disbelief.

As he removed the garter belt and stockings, he recalled how sexy he found it when women wore them. How strange to be removing them from his own body! *Am I sexy?*

He washed his face clean of makeup, feeling more himself. Needing to take a piss, he raised the toilet seat and reached down to grab himself, but found empty air. Momentarily puzzled, he then lowered the seat and sat down to do his business.

Curious, he gazed at his groin and touched his pubic hair. Hana had shaved herself into a neat cut. He ran his fingers over his mound then used both hands to separate the labia. He reached between his legs and felt his vaginal opening, then inserted a bit of his middle finger. Yes, he had a vagina. He was a woman. This was all too, too weird — he had to get his own body back. He stood and faced the mirror, searching for some sign of himself in Hana's features.

How old was Hana? He couldn't remember the birth date on the driver's license, but figured she must be around thirty. He wondered about her being a prostitute. Was Marvin her pimp? How much of a cut did she have to give him? If she was selling herself for sex, could she not find other work?

Then again, she could be an escort. In his mind, the word *escort* designated a service much classier and more expensive, not that he knew anything about such things. He had never frequented such people and had never paid for sex. He sometimes wondered if he had missed a life experience, but these days, with talk of STDs and HIV, it seemed like the risk far outweighed the reward. Why take a chance for a moment of pleasure and end up paying dearly, even with one's life? Should everybody be walking around with official documentation of their latest health test to prove to a potential partner they were infection-free? While it all seemed practical, it also seemed to take the eroticism out of a spontaneous act of lust.

Alan cupped his breasts. He moved his hands over them, lifted them, and let them bounce. Here he was on the other side of the sexual divide, no longer admiring tits but possessing a pair — not his own, exactly, but for the moment this body was his. He shook his head. *Focus!* He had to get back to the matter at hand.

In a bureau, he found Hana's undergarments. They all seemed to be black, and he wondered if this was due to her career or personal preference. Holding up a lacy black bra, he frowned. How in the hell was he was going to get this thing on? His first attempt was to go about it the way he'd seen women do it, but fiddling behind his back with the catches had him cursing in no time. Craning his neck to get a glimpse in the mirror of what his hands were doing also proved fruitless. Finally, he tackled it in the most logical way: he did the bra up with the clasp in front and slid it around into the correct position before getting his arms through the straps. The lace felt silky against his skin, but the bra itself felt tight and he wondered if he had got something wrong.

He put on the jeans and shirt he had chosen earlier and hunted around for other footwear. There were loafers on the floor of the closet. This would make it easier to get across town and back to his condo.

A cookie jar sat on top of the bureau. It seemed out of place, but it looked to him like the sort of knickknack a woman would add to dress things up. Inside, he found a bank book and fourteen hundred dollars in small bills. On the back was a small sticky note showing a four-digit number, which he guessed was the PIN for the account. Her checking account showed a balance of twenty-two thousand dollars. Was that all the money she had?

Something else caught his eye. He reached into the jar again and pulled out an envelope marked *Tayport Wealth Management.* He unfolded the pages and read the heading *Personal Investment Portfolio* before scanning down a list of various funds: a total of four hundred and fifteen thousand dollars. He paused, startled by the amount, and wondered again who this Hana was and how he and she were connected.

After putting everything back in the cookie jar, he walked back into the main room looking around for other places to investigate. The fridge was spotted with magnets, one of which held a piece of paper. It was a notice for an appointment at the Neuroscience Establishment. He'd been there the morning before, volunteering for an experiment. This was a link between himself and this woman. He had to get back to his condo to see what other pieces of the puzzle he could find.

As he went around and switched off the lights, he noticed it was coming up to one a.m. It had been an eventful night, and it wasn't over yet. Just as Alan reached for the door, a buzzer sounded. He scanned the room and his eyes fell upon a wall-mounted phone system. He walked over and examined the device; the buzzer sounded again. He pushed a button marked *View.* A small screen lit up and showed what he guessed was the front door of the building. There was a man standing there — it was Marvin.

Alan decided this was neither the time nor the place to deal with the man. He locked up, headed down the hall in the opposite direction, and left through a back exit.

Chapter 3

Alan couldn't find a taxi, so he headed to a subway station. He figured he was half an hour away from getting some answers.

Boarding a nearly empty subway car, he gazed into space, lost in thought. There were a thousand questions and few answers. This certainly couldn't be a dream. *Shouldn't I have woken up by now?*

As he looked down the length of the car, movement disturbed his musings. Halfway down, a man stood at one of the doors, staring at him with a mischievous grin. Alan blinked. He could see the man, but didn't register what he was seeing. He blinked again as realization dawned — the man was openly masturbating.

Alan gawked in disbelief. Years ago, Christy, a good friend of his, had recounted her run-in with a man who had exposed himself on the subway. While the whole story had seemed ludicrous, she had felt threatened by this public sex act. Nothing had happened to her, and Alan discovered later that most of the time people who expose themselves are looking for a thrill, for a reaction, rather than wanting sex with their audience.

Nevertheless, he had a visceral response to this man's behavior. He didn't feel threatened so much as intruded upon: this man had invaded his space. It angered him. *Jack off if you want to, but don't shove it in my face.*

He stood up and walked toward the man who continued to stroke himself. However, his smile gave way to a questioning look — he clearly hadn't expected Alan to come forward.

Alan stopped about ten feet from the man. "You know, my Chihuahua has a bigger dick than that." He pointed to the man's groin.

The man looked panicked. He frantically tried to stuff his penis back into his pants and fled to the far end of the subway car. When the doors opened, the man shot a parting glance down the car and hurried off the train. Alan went back to where he had been.

"Idiot," he muttered.

A prerecorded voice announced his stop. There wasn't a bus in sight, so Alan walked the six blocks to his condo. Rounding the last corner, he looked up at the complex, which loomed behind a line of commercial buildings. A light on in his living room meant he was close to some answers. He entered the building vestibule and brushed his shoes on the rug out of habit before walking through the next doors into the lobby. He strode up to the security desk and said, "Good evening, Bobby."

The man blinked. "Sorry, do I know you?"

Alan realized his mistake and smiled. "I'm Hana Toussaint. I'm here to visit Alan Maitland in suite eight twelve."

"Is he expecting you?"

"Sort of. He may be surprised."

Bobby picked up the phone. "Just a moment. I'll ring him."

Alan leaned on the desk and attempted to look nonchalant — as if this were all normal. The security guard exchanged a few words over the phone then turned to Alan.

"Mr. Maitland would like to speak to you."

He took the phone. "Hello, Alan? It's Hana Toussaint. I thought I would pop over for that discussion we need to have."

There was a moment of silence, and then he heard his own voice say, "Hana?"

"Yes, Alan. It's Hana. Buzz me through and I'll come right up." He handed the phone back.

Bobby pointed to the far side of the lobby. "Go through those doors and take the elevator to the eighth floor."

Alan gave him a bright smile. "Thank you."

Once on his floor, he tried the handle on the first door on the left. It was locked. He knocked and said, "Open up."

Something flickered in the peephole. Impatient, he knocked again. "Come on, open up." There was another moment of silence, then the click of the lock. He grabbed the handle and swung the door open as he charged into his apartment. He shut the door, locked it, and flicked on the overhead light with a practiced movement. Alan spun around to find himself face to face with himself. His gut clenched. This wasn't a dream; this was real.

"You're Hana, aren't you," he said.

She gawked at him. "Yes." She looked him up and down before reaching out a tentative hand grazing his shoulder. "Are you me? Am I you?"

He tossed her purse on the countertop. "Let's sit down and figure this out."

Alan walked into the open area past his glass dining table and plopped himself in one of the four armchairs arranged around his coffee table. Hana slowly came forward, still staring at him. He pointed to an armchair across from him. "Sit down."

She did as he told.

"I take it you're a prostitute."

She crossed her arms defensively. "Well ... yes."

"What happened to you?"

She hesitated. "I ... I was with someone. Then I wasn't. I found myself here in bed. I wandered around trying to figure out what was going on — and then I looked at myself in the mirror."

He smirked. "You were 'with someone'? That's putting it mildly! I took your place and found myself performing oral sex on a guy named Mr. Smith."

She chuckled.

"I didn't think it was funny," Alan said. "After I gagged and asked him to stop, your Mr. Smith insisted on continuing."

"Oh, he's such a nice man. He's been married for decades and loves his wife, but she refuses to perform oral sex on him. Every once in a while, he comes to me to give himself a treat."

"I punched him in the balls."

"You did *what?*" Her eyes widened, and her hand fluttered to her mouth.

"I wouldn't suck his dick. He kept insisting, and I couldn't think of any other way to convince him I was serious. That brought things to a dead halt."

"Oh my God. He's one of my regular clients, a charming man!" Her voice was forceful. "Did you have to be so rough?"

"Did I have a choice? He thought I was you!"

She wavered. "I guess."

"Then Marvin showed up."

"What? Why?"

"Your Mr. Smith phoned him, apparently."

"Yes, I give the number of my answering service to my clients."

"So, who is this Marvin? Your pimp?"

"For heaven's sake, no," she said. "I work independently. Marvin's security at the hotel and moonlights as protection for various girls. I hire him periodically as a driver and as a bodyguard if I'm working with a new client."

Alan avoided looking at her. "I was ... uh, confused, a little scared, and I ..."

Hana's tone went up. "Good Lord, what did you do?"

"I used your stun gun on him."

She slumped forward and massaged her forehead with one hand. "Oh ... my ... God ..."

"Maybe I shouldn't have done that."

"You think? How much damage to my reputation can one man do in so short of a time?"

"What? I had no idea what was going on. Hell, I didn't even understand I wasn't in my own body." Alan too rubbed his forehead and let out a sigh. *What a night.* "I noticed on your fridge—"

"You found my apartment?" Her head jerked.

"The address is on your driver's license."

"Oh."

"You had an appointment yesterday at the Neuroscience Establishment." He paused. "Why did you go there?"

"I saw a notice requesting volunteers for the test program of a new brain–computer interface. A cousin of mine lost an arm in an accident years ago, and he's been involved in BCI tests for an artificial arm. I made some inquiries and discovered this technology is a new approach to BCI." She took a deep breath. "Instead of electrodes attached to the head, the type of interface my cousin worked with, this interface involved a subcutaneous chip. I was so intrigued that I signed up. A research assistant named Kyle scanned my brain using a helmet-like contraption then inserted what he called a BCI chip in the back of my neck. Over the next week, I was to participate in various experiments under the direction of a Doctor Blackmore."

Alan touched the back of his neck. "Me, too." *So much for wanting to be a nice guy and volunteering ...*

"Really? I don't remember seeing you."

"I had the scan in the morning but had to rush to a meeting, so I went back for the chip insertion late in the afternoon."

"So what happened? How did our minds get switched?"

"I have no idea," Alan said. "Why would anybody want us to switch bodies? What purpose does that serve? Nobody would do this for a lark. There has to be an objective."

"I'm nobody important. Are you?"

He looked away and rubbed his chin. "I sometimes think I am, when I have a bout of arrogance, but in the grand scheme of things? Not really."

Hana tilted her head. "What do you do?"

"I work for an investment firm."

As the two of them sat in silence, Alan's mind raced, more confused than ever. He had come for answers but had only ended up with more questions.

He sighed. "It's the middle of the night. We're not going to solve anything until morning."

"Aren't you scared?"

"I suppose I should be, but right now I'm more pissed than anything else. This is a major inconvenience. I've enough going on in my life, and I don't need any more problems to deal with."

She leaned forward on her elbows. "I'm scared."

"I'd like to say 'don't be,' but I have no idea what's going on. I don't know the extent of the problem or what possible solutions exist." He sighed again. "I don't know about you, but I'm beat. This has been an exhausting night."

"This was more excitement than I was counting on."

He stood. "Oh, I don't think your excitement will be over anytime soon."

"Why do you say that?"

"Marvin showed up at your apartment. I'm sure he's pissed about me stunning him."

She stared up at him askance. "Did you talk with him?"

"No. I saw who it was on your video security, so I left by the back exit. I think you'll have to make amends to both Mr. Smith and Marvin."

Alan headed toward his bedroom. "I'm going to take a shower. You get the guest room."

Hana got up and went after him. "Wait. What do you mean, 'amends'?"

He stopped and turned around. "I punched your client in the nuts. I tased your security guy. The longer I stay in this body, the more trouble I'm going to make for you."

She exhaled slowly. "This experience is turning into a life changer."

"I think both of us have already suffered a major life change. Can it get any worse than ending up in somebody else's body?"

"Okay, but I don't think my body is that bad." She gave a little pout.

"You know what I mean: I'm a man, and you're a woman. I think it would be better if our bodies matched our genders."

He continued down the hall and gestured to the guest room. "It's all yours. Guest bathroom across the hall. Help yourself."

He disappeared into the master bedroom.

After he switched on the light, Alan went to his walk-in closet and studied the hangers. This was his condo and these were his clothes, but this wasn't his body. Nothing would fit; he'd have to buy other things or retrieve more clothes from Hana's apartment. For now, he'd rinse out the panties and socks then figure something out tomorrow. He was beat and needed to sleep.

He stripped off his clothes and left them on a chair. As the hot water washed over him, he felt a bit of the day's stress melt away. After sticking his head under the nozzle to get his head wet, he washed his hair. Even though his eyes were shut, he could feel the change in air pressure as the shower door opened.

"Hana? What are you doing?"

"I thought I could wash my back." She giggled. "And I thought you could wash yours."

As he continued to wash his hair, he thought how strange it was to hear his own voice. "I don't need any help," he said. "Besides, let's not make this any more complicated than it already is."

"You're in pretty good shape."

"Thanks. I work out regularly. Now how about you use the other shower?" He finished rinsing the soap out of his hair and bumped flush up against Hana. They held each other's gaze.

"What are you doing?" He pointed to the door. "Get out."

She shrugged. "I felt a certain intimacy. I always try to get into a guy's head, but this is the first time I've gotten into his body."

He reached for the soap and brushed up against her. He glanced down. She had an erection.

"Oh, Christ!" He jumped out of the way. "You're kidding me! You have a hard-on? Seriously?"

"It's *your* body," she said, nonchalant. "Although, it seems kind of erotic to be a guy."

He glared at her. "I guess I haven't taken the time to mull over the implications of switching genders. Now, if you don't mind, get out." He opened the door and pushed her out of the shower. "And don't tell me you have fantasies about making love to yourself."

She stuck her head back in the shower. "Why not? I do it all the time." She grinned mischievously.

Alan put his hand on her forehead and pushed her firmly

out of the way, then finished his shower in peace.

After rinsing out his undergarments by hand, he went down the hall and put them in the dryer. They would be fine in the morning.

On the way back, he stopped outside the guest room. "I forgot," he said as he peeked in. "There's a spare toothbrush and toothpaste under the sink."

Hana stood naked in front of the mirror holding up both arms and flexing her muscles. "I found them. Thanks."

"What are you doing?"

"I'm impressed by your physique. Most of the men I see are middle-aged and not in the best shape. You take care of yourself." She ran a hand over her stomach, admiring her abs in the mirror.

"I try. I work out regularly. I think everybody should." He yawned. "I have to hit the hay. I'm exhausted. Tomorrow, we go to the clinic."

"Okay."

"Good night." He went to his room and shut the door, his mind racing through everything that had happened. His entire life had been upended, and he felt on the verge of losing control. He tried to remain calm and rationally manage the situation step by step, but now this odd woman was making things even more bizarre.

He ambled to the bed and noticed his smartphone on the nightstand. *Geez, the meeting* ... He sent a message to the office coordinator explaining that he was sick and wouldn't be coming in to work. That should buy him some time. He slid between the sheets and rolled onto one side, trying to put everything out of his mind. Tomorrow would be a busy day.

Alan was drifting off to sleep when the bed bounced. He tensed. "Hana?"

There was a moment of silence then a voice in the darkness said, "Yes?"

"What are you doing?"

"It's a queen-size bed. I thought I could sleep here."

There was another moment of silence. Alan rolled onto his

back. "What exactly do you think is going to happen here?"

Hana giggled.

"This is too weird," Alan said.

"Why? Haven't you ever kissed a boy before?"

"Listen, I've got nothing against homosexuality, but I discovered a long time ago which team I prefer. You could say I'm a flaming heterosexual. Besides, that's not the issue."

She rolled onto her side and faced him, head propped up in one hand. "No? I've kissed a girl."

"In your line of work, I wouldn't be surprised. Nevertheless, I would appreciate it if you would go back to the guest room."

"I have no idea how you could sleep after everything that's happened." She moved her hands over the sheets. "Besides, this bed's nicer."

Alan took a deep breath. "No offense, but I have no idea of your health status. If anything were to happen, I would want to see documentation of recent tests."

"I get tested regularly. I'm clean. Plus, I always practice safe sex."

"It didn't seem so safe when you were performing oral sex on that guy."

"I had put a condom on him. Didn't you notice?"

An unwelcome image came to Alan's mind. "Oh, right. I think I might have been a tad distracted by finding a cock shoved down my throat."

She chuckled. "You need to learn how to relax your throat muscles and overcome the gag reflex."

"That isn't on my to-do list."

"I can show you, if you want."

"Thanks but no thanks. What would the neighbors think if they found out I had gone down on myself?"

She giggled again. "See? You *do* have a sense of humor about this."

"I suppose. But walking around as a woman has been an eye-opener."

"What do you mean?"

"Men seem to be attracted to you, and if they're not staring, they're being crude. A guy exposed himself to me on the subway."

The bed vibrated slightly as Hana tried to stifle a guffaw. "That's a woman's world. Guys can be something else."

"What happened to politeness, respect, or even common decency? Some young punk said out loud that he wanted to fuck me."

"Yup. It would be a step up if they would say 'please' when they say they want to fuck a woman. Unfortunately, some men seem to have a sense of entitlement and treat women as second-class citizens. I'm just a sex toy who can vote."

"You need another line of work."

"Oh, don't get me wrong — not all men are pigs. Some of my clients are real gentlemen. Yes, sex is involved, but they appreciate good service, and I give them something they can't get elsewhere."

"Elsewhere?"

"Like at home from their wives. Sometimes these men want a blowjob. Sometimes they want somebody to listen to them. They want to feel important. They want to be desired, to be appreciated. They want to feel like a man."

"Your description doesn't seem very flattering of marriage."

"Traditional marriages aren't always the best. I think society dictates to men and women the roles they have to play. So instead of being open and honest, many men and women do what they think they're supposed to do, and that leads to unfulfilled lives. People ultimately look for fulfillment elsewhere."

"You seem to be a bit of a psychologist and poetic observer of life."

"I have a bachelor of arts with a major in psychology."

"You do?"

"Yes."

"Color me duly impressed."

"Just because I'm a sex worker doesn't mean I'm stupid. Or uneducated."

Alan paused, realizing how judgmental he was. "Sorry."

"I get that a lot. We live in a puritanical society, and people look down on sex: it's bad, it's disgusting, and anybody who does it — especially anybody who does it for money — is also bad and disgusting. Quite a shame, really. Sex is wonderful, and can be beautiful under the right circumstances. We humans, for some ungodly reason, love to screw things up." She chuckled. "Yep, we screw up our screwing."

They lay silently in the darkness. "I must give you more credit," Alan said.

"For what?"

"I didn't know what to expect from you. You seem wiser than I would have assumed."

"Most men are interested in whether or not I'm a good fuck. They don't all take the time to find out that I have a head on my shoulders and I like to think I have a pretty good head." She leaned over and spoke softly into his ear: "I have a good head, and I *give* good head."

"Let's get some sleep." He turned onto his side and forced himself to stop thinking.

Chapter 4

Alan woke from a deep sleep. It took a moment to grasp where he was and to become aware of his surroundings. A male arm draped over his chest. Then he realized a body was spooning him. While these two pieces of information would have normally made him jump out of bed, his brain slowly recalled the events of the previous night. He wasn't in bed with a man; he was in bed with a *woman*. It was a woman in a man's body, *his* body, but she was a she. Alan wasn't awake enough to either chuckle or freak out.

Hana seemed to be still asleep. He shifted and felt something pressing against his buttocks. He rolled his eyes; she had a morning erection. That is, *he* had a morning erection, or at least his body had one. Their minds had been switched. For some reason, Alan thought that sounded like a 1950s black and white horror film: *Revenge of the Transferred Minds*, in CinemaScope.

He carefully lifted Hana's arm off him and slid out of bed. The clock read seven forty-five. He patiently stood in front of the coffee machine until the whooshing noise announced his morning jolt of caffeine. As he raised his cup to savor that first sip, he gazed out the living-room windows to the city lit by the rays of the morning sun.

The patter of bare feet in the hall caught his attention. Hana, wearing a robe, walked into the kitchen, stretched, and said, "Good morning. I didn't hear you get up."

"Can I get you a coffee?"

"I'd prefer tea if you have it."

He opened a cupboard above the brewer. "I have an assortment of just about everything."

"No pot of coffee? Single servings? Seems decadent."

"I suppose. But when you live by yourself, this is easier and involves less waste."

She examined the labels, then removed a pack from a box marked *Earl Grey*. "You live by yourself? No wife? Girlfriend?"

"Life is busy right now." He held out a cup. "There's milk

if you want."

"Thanks. I like it black."

Alan took a seat in an armchair. "Let's work out a plan of action."

She followed him. "You're definitely a businessman."

"Why do you say that?"

"Oh, plan of action, a classy apartment, a one-cup brewer ... You seem to be a businessman — someone who goes around making decisions."

"I suppose. Doesn't everybody?"

"Yes, but most of us make decisions that affect nobody but ourselves."

He sipped his coffee. "We'll grab a bite and head over to the clinic. I want to find out what connection there could be to our mutual experience."

Alan's landline rang.

He walked to the kitchen counter and picked up the receiver. "Hello?" He listened a moment then put his hand over the mouthpiece. Eyes wide, he said, "Hana, come here! I keep forgetting I'm you, not me. Work's calling, and I need you to talk to somebody."

"Okay." She put down her cup and ran over.

He continued to hold his hand over the receiver as he dug a pad of paper and a pen out of a drawer. "You talk, and I'll coach you on what to say. I'm going to put this on speaker, so I can listen. Remember, your name's Alan Maitland." He took a breath. "Ready?"

She nodded. He pressed a button and put the receiver in its cradle.

A voice issued from the speaker. "Hello? Is anybody there?"

Alan whispered into Hana's ear: "His name is Jack."

She said aloud, "Jack, hello."

There was a moment of silence. "You have me on speaker?"

Alan held up a note that read, "Making breakfast."

"Uh, sorry. I'm making breakfast," she said.

"Had a late night? I see you have company," Jack said.

Hana looked unsure of what to say. "Yeah."

"Barbara told me you emailed saying you wouldn't be in today. Are you actually sick or did you tie one on last night?"

Hana gave Alan a questioning look.

"Listen," Jack continued, "we were supposed to have a preliminary planning session with Fred this morning at ten thirty. What do you want me to tell him?"

Alan cupped his hand over Hana's ear and whispered, "It's not urgent. Put it off until next week."

She spoke into the phone. "It's not urgent, Jack. Put it off until next week."

"Okay. You're the boss. I hope you're feeling better." Jack cleared his throat. "Give my regards to the ... *nurse*." Alan heard Jack chuckle before the call was terminated.

"Whew, that was close," Hana said.

"Yes, but you did a good job. This situation is going to become more and more problematic. Even though you have my body, you don't have my knowledge or experience. You can't do my job. You can't answer questions. You don't know people. I'm sure that anybody who knows me would think I've lost my mind."

"I guess the same is true for me."

"I'd say so. I would think that each of us has a limited amount of time to trick people before they realize something's wrong."

"Hmm. I know my clients would wonder why I stopped giving blowjobs all of a sudden."

He gave her a sarcastic look.

"And no deep throat," she added.

He shook his head. "Okay, okay. You've made your point. We both have unique skill sets."

She put a hand on his shoulder and gave him a look that was both playful and seductive. "You may make more money than me, but I'm sure I leave people with more smiles than you."

Alan looked at Hana and thought her attempt at being sexy

probably came across better when she was a woman. This was a curious switch. *Do my masculine mannerisms look odd coming from a woman?*

"Ha ha," he said without humor. "Let's get dressed and grab a bagel on our way to the clinic." He started for his bedroom. "I'll pick out some clothes for you."

As Alan grabbed socks and underwear, he handed them to Hana. He picked out a blue shirt and a dark two-piece suit for her to wear. Looking over a rack of ties, he picked something in a deep shade of red with a subtle design. "Put those on. I'll do the tie."

"Do you always dress so formally?"

"Formally?" He shrugged. "Just trying to look decent. It *is* a normal business day, after all."

"Can we stop at my apartment?"

"Why?"

"If you're going to look decent, I think I should look decent too. Do you want to run around in jeans and no makeup while I'm dressed up in a suit? Not a good image."

"Point taken."

"Besides, my apartment is on the way to the Neuroscience Establishment and I do have clothes that are dressier."

"Oh?"

"Come off it! Do you think I go around dressed like I was last night all the time? I have a life, you know."

"Okay, you get dressed, and then we'll head out." He stopped. "By the way, think you know how to use an electric razor?"

"What?" She rubbed her chin. "I'll be darned — stubble." She brushed a hand against her cheek. "I'll give it a go."

"And I'll get you my skin lotion — I don't use any of those fancy colognes. Oh yeah, and my deodorant."

The two of them went about their business, with Alan sticking his head in twice to ask if she needed any assistance. Thirty minutes later, Hana walked out just as Alan knotted the tie he'd picked out for her around his own neck.

He looked her up and down. "You clean up rather well, Ms.

Toussaint. Or should I say Mr. Maitland?" He expanded the loop of the tie and pulled it off.

She smiled, held on to each side of the suit jacket, and curtseyed. "Why, thank you."

He pursed his lips. "You should consider nodding your head, or pumping your fist and saying, *All right!*"

"I'm not sure I'm going to get this guy thing. Then again, do I want to?"

"We both have our work cut out for us."

"Of course, I *do* run into the occasional customer who likes me to play the dominant and—"

Alan held up a hand. "Too much information." He stepped closer to look at Hana's neckline. "Put your shirt collar up and do up your top button."

She did so and feigned gagging.

"Funny." He handed her the tie. "Slip this over your head." He adjusted the loop around her neck then held the knot and pulled the short end until it was in place. "Put the collar down."

He looked at the results and centered the knot. "There. You look professional."

"Thanks." She turned and looked at herself in a mirror, tilting her head left and right. "Not bad." Grabbing the long end of the tie, she held it over her head and gagged again, crossing her eyes.

"Aren't *you* the card." He gathered up his phone and keys and put them in the purse. "I must say, you gals have a great idea here with these purses. We guys are always looking for a spare pocket, and not all items are small enough."

"Is that a cellphone or are you happy to see me?"

He gave her a droll look. "Let's go." He took a step to the door and stopped. "What are you doing?" She had a hand in one pocket fumbling around. "This is no time for pocket pool," he said.

"I'm uncomfortable!"

"You have to get your testicles in the front part of the briefs with the penis pointing up."

"This is a pain. I always thought you dirty little boys were jerking off in public. Who knew you have to keep adjusting the family jewels?"

Alan sighed. "Put your hand down your waistband and just do it — we haven't got all day. And be gentle, for God's sake. That's *my* junk you're playing around with." He held the door open to let her pass and flicked off the lights. "I had an amusing thought," he said, locking the door.

"Oh?" Hana said as they strode toward the elevator.

"Since you're the man and I'm the woman, you should hold the door for me." He pushed the button.

She giggled.

He gave her a critical look. "That laugh isn't ..."

"Isn't what?"

"Isn't something I would do."

"What? Now you want me to *laugh* differently?"

"Maybe in a more masculine way."

"And how would you classify a laugh as more masculine?"

He was trying to think of something to say when the elevator pinged and the doors opened. "Let me think about it."

They stepped in to find another couple. Alan and Hana nodded to them and turned to face the closing doors.

She put an arm around his shoulders and leaned over to kiss him on the cheek. He stiffened. She spoke in a quiet voice: "You were fantastic last night."

Alan heard the woman behind him trying to stifle a chuckle. He pictured the man grinning. A flush rose to his cheeks as he watched the floor numbers pass by.

As soon as the doors to the elevator opened, he exited the car and strode purposefully across the lobby. Hana had to half walk, half skip to keep up with him.

The morning security guard looked up from his desk and called out, "Have a good day, Mr. Maitland."

"Thanks, André," Alan said.

André gave Alan a surprised look then regarded Hana. The other couple entered the lobby and distracted him.

Alan pushed open the outer doors, checked for traffic, and

walked across the street. Hana jogged to catch up.

"What's the matter?" She smiled. "It's a beautiful day."

He stopped abruptly with his hands on his hips. "Would you mind toning it down a notch? I like to think I have a good reputation in my building."

She grinned. "If they only knew what you were doing last night ..."

He opened his mouth to say something, thought better of it, and continued down the street in a huff.

She hurried after him. "Aw, come on — that was funny."

Chapter 5

Alan and Hana approached her building. "The man at the top of the front steps," she whispered, "is the super. Call him Harvey."

As they went up the steps, Alan said, "Hi Harvey."

The balding man stopped sweeping the entrance of the building and looked up. "Hana, may I have a word?"

Hana and Alan stopped. "Yes? Oh—" Alan gestured to Hana. "This is Alan, a friend of mine."

"In private?" Harvey turned to Hana. "No offense."

"Don't worry — Alan's a good friend. You can say anything in front of him."

Harvey glanced at Hana, then back at Alan. "Okay. Some guy by the name of Marvin buzzed me in the middle of the night."

"What?" Alan endeavored to look surprised.

"He told me you were behaving oddly, and he was concerned about you. He came around to see you, but you didn't answer. He insisted I check up on you."

"What happened?" Hana said.

"I let him in, and the two of us went up to your apartment. I knocked several times then unlocked the door to see if you were there or not. Obviously, you weren't." Harvey leaned on his broom. "I'm not supposed to go into people's apartments without permission, but this guy was so worried about you. Who *is* this Marvin?"

Alan glanced at Hana.

"He's a business associate," Hana said. "I appreciate his concern. *We* appreciate his concern. Hana wasn't feeling like herself last night, and ... well, it's nice to know somebody cares."

Harvey gave her a curious look. "You seem like a close friend, Alan. How odd I've never seen you before."

"Not all of my friends visit me here," Alan said. "I'm so sorry for the inconvenience, Harvey. I'll do my best to rectify things with Marvin."

"I'm glad you're okay. Take care of yourself." He returned to his sweeping.

Inside, Alan pushed open the door of Hana's apartment. "Listen, I'm sorry."

"It's not your fault."

"I may have overreacted last night."

She shrugged. "How are you supposed to react when you find yourself in somebody else's body?"

"Yeah. So, you said you had some professional-looking clothes for me?"

"Follow me."

In the bedroom, he watched as she went through a chest of drawers and the closet, arranging pieces on the bed.

"There," she said. "This should do the trick. And while you're getting dressed, I'll catch up on some of my own business." She walked out of the bedroom.

"Thanks." Alan undid one button of his blouse, shutting the bedroom door out of habit. He stopped — that was a ridiculous thing to do. This was *her* body. He was hiding it from its rightful owner.

Alan stripped everything off and put on the clothing Hana had selected. He didn't bother to struggle with the right way to do the bra again, putting it on backward and sliding it around instead. Success was more important than style. He sat down on the edge of the bed and bunched up a leg of the pantyhose before pulling it over his foot. He paused then ran a hand up and down his leg. "Am I supposed to be shaving my legs?" he called to Hana.

"Considering your expertise is with an electric razor, I'm not sure I'd let you loose in the same room with my body and my regular razor," she called back. "The pantyhose will let you fake it until we figure out what we're doing."

He raised his left arm and looked at his underarm before running his hand through the armpit. He shrugged and continued pulling on the pantyhose. After getting both legs to his thighs, he stood up and pulled the hose up over his hips. He stood for a moment then took a few steps. The sensation of having his legs encased in nylon was new. He ran his hands up and down his thighs. It was a curious feeling, but good.

"Pantyhose?" he asked. "No garter belt?"

"Not all the time — although that seems to be a favorite with you guys."

With you guys? What a curious idea: a woman who catered to the needs and pleasures of men. What did Hana truly know about the needs and pleasures of men? Did she understand all their little kinks, perversions, and idiosyncrasies? He had heard of high-priced escorts making tens of thousands of dollars. *Why do women become sex workers? Why do men frequent sex workers?* But what did he know about any of this?

He walked into the living room holding a pair of shoes. "You want me to wear these?" He held them up, examining the short heels.

She glanced up from her laptop. "Yes, silly. They match the outfit perfectly. They're almost flat, so they're much more comfortable and easier to walk in. You'll see."

"Oh, good. I have no idea how you gals walk in heels. What a pain in the butt!"

She shrugged. "You boys love seeing us all gussied up and sexy."

"Yes, but until last night, I had never appreciated the precariousness of trying to balance myself on stilettos. Hell, you're taking your life in your hands in those things."

She chuckled. "True. Oh, the things we women go through to get your attention."

"Really?"

She gave Alan a knowing smile. "You men are visual. Everything works in your eyes before it works in your brain — or should I say, before it works in your groin."

"I guess."

"Guess? It's my *job* to know."

"You paint an unflattering portrait of men as one-dimensional creatures."

Hana laughed again. "Don't get me wrong — I like men. You have a singularity of purpose I both admire and love. Any woman loves feeling as if she's the center of the universe, the focus of a man's attention. It's just that your hormones sometimes go into overdrive and suppress all upper brain functions. That happens to women too, but not in the same way. In any case, I do so love the animal in you."

"You do?"

"Alan, women don't want just to be loved — they want to be desired, craved, and lusted after. They want that primordial connection with another human being as much as any man does."

"Primordial?" He looked at her with a raised eyebrow.

"I read, you know. I'm not stupid."

"Never mind the language. You seem to have a more profound understanding of the human condition than I first thought."

"Oh?" She cocked her head. "You mean you might have had some preconceived notions about me?"

"I ... well ..." He lowered his head. "Yes."

"If society didn't vilify sex work, it would be considered the same as any other job. You can pay for a massage, and nobody says anything. A massage makes you feel good, loosens your muscles, and eases pain. A good orgasm can do the same thing. Who got up on their high horse and decided a massage is okay but an orgasm isn't?"

"Well ..."

"Sorry, you shouldn't get me started. I get ticked off at being looked down upon because I have sex for money. It's the double standard: men can have sex left, right, and center and are considered manly. If a woman has sex, she's a slut."

"I think I saw evidence of that last night."

"I recommend that every man spend some time as a woman. It would open their eyes to the injustices in our society, a society that's patriarchal. What's that saying I read the other day? Oh yeah: If men got pregnant, abortions would be available at every corner store." She laughed. "You're a man — you have advantages I don't. But now you're a woman. You can experience first-hand what I have to go through daily."

She went back to typing.

"I may have got more than I bargained for," Alan said. "Life as a woman can be difficult."

"You know what they say, of course." She smiled slyly. "Life's a bitch. If it was a slut, it would be easy."

Alan nodded and chuckled. "Shall we go?"

"Just a sec." She hit a few keys then looked at her hands. "It's kind of nice, typing without long fingernails." She squinted at the screen, positioned her hands, and typed in a flurry.

He perused the room. "I saw your portfolio statement."

"You're quite the snoop."

"I was merely trying to figure out what was going on. I wasn't intentionally prying into your affairs."

"No matter."

"I'm impressed."

"You mean you're surprised."

"Okay, that too." He followed her fingers then said, "You have quite the portfolio."

She stopped typing and clicked her tongue. "I'm at the peak of my career. I'm frugal. I save. And I invest prudently and wisely. I'm not going to do this forever, and if I'm to have a future in which I'm in any way financially independent, I have to depend on myself. I'm not looking for a sugar daddy, and I'm not looking to get married. I don't expect a prince to rescue me. This is my show, and I'm going to do it my way." She went back to her work.

He stood there looking at her, wondering what to say.

She hit the final key with a flourish and shut the laptop. "Done." Then she studied him. "How about we brush your hair and put on a little makeup?"

"Makeup? Aw jeez, do I have to?"

She shook her head. "What a crybaby! Well, Mr. Bigshot, you can just man up — or should I say woman up — and get with the program."

She took his arm and led him to the bathroom. She opened a cabinet drawer and laid out various items beside the sink punctuating her movement with a word for each item. "Moisturizer. Foundation. Concealer. Blush. Mascara. Eye shadow. Lipstick."

He clicked his tongue in disgust. "This has got to be a joke."

"I'll make a woman out of you yet." She giggled again.

She picked up a bottle and held it out to him. "First, the moisturizer."

He looked at it warily. "I'm not going to end up looking like I did last night?"

"That was full-blown war paint. Today calls for subtlety and professionalism."

He reluctantly took the bottle and pointed to the mascara. "I just know I'm going to poke an eye out."

"I'm here to help. You'll be a pro in no time."

It took some time, some back and forth, and some chuckling on her part at his clumsiness. In the end, he grudgingly admitted that it looked good. He turned his head from side to side examining his face in the mirror.

"I do know what I'm doing," she said.

He nodded. "Okay. Now can we go? I'm dying for something to eat."

"Fine. There's a coffee shop on the way to the clinic."

"Good. One step closer to sorting this mess out."

Chapter 6

Alan and Hana crossed the main foyer of the New York Development Center and rode an elevator to the ninth floor. With exaggerated politeness, Hana held the door bearing the name *The Neuroscience Establishment*, and Alan entered first. They traversed a small waiting room and stood before the reception desk.

"Good morning," Alan said.

The middle-aged woman behind the counter concentrated on her computer screen. She finished typing and looked up, first at Alan then at Hana. "May I help you?"

"We'd like to speak with Kyle," Alan said.

The woman gave him a look of incomprehension. "Kyle?"

"Yes. We both had appointments with Kyle yesterday and we're interested in following up with him."

The woman stood up. "I don't think we have a Kyle working here."

"That's the name of the guy we saw." Alan glanced at Hana. "Isn't that so?"

Hana nodded.

The woman gave Hana a questioning look. "Are you sure you're in the right place?"

"Yes, *I'm* sure," Alan said.

"Just a second. Let me ask somebody else." The receptionist took two steps then stopped and turned to look at Hana. "May I say who's inquiring?"

"Alan Maitland," Hana said.

The woman disappeared through another door. Alan curled his lip and frowned as he stared after her.

Hana leaned closer. "How did you hear about this BCI test?"

"My uncle had Lou Gehrig's disease for the last ten years of his life and participated in a BCI pilot program. An old friend, James Channon, is involved in funding BCI research at the university and told me about this test. He thought I would want to contribute something to the cause." He idly tapped the countertop. "How did *you* hear about it?"

"I volunteer twice a month at the hospital."

"You do?"

"Yes. I like to give something back to the community. Anyway, I saw a notice pinned up on a bulletin board in the main reception area."

The receptionist came back, followed by a thirty-something man dressed in a lab coat. "Billy will answer your questions," she said.

"Thank you," Alan said.

"If you'll follow me," Billy said, "we can find ourselves some privacy." He led them down the hall to an examination room. "Have a seat."

Billy sat facing Hana across a small table that served as a desk. "How can I help you?"

"We'd like some information," Alan said.

Billy glanced at Alan then back to Hana. "You told the receptionist you had appointments here with somebody called Kyle?"

Alan said, "*I* told the receptionist we had appointments."

"Oh, I see." Billy looked at Hana. "You are?"

Hana said, "Alan Maitland."

Alan glared at Billy who continued speaking to Hana. "So you and Mrs. Maitland came in yesterday."

"Yes," Hana said.

"We're not married," Alan said.

Billy smiled.

Hana put a hand on Alan's knee. "Now, dear ..." She gave Billy a shrug. "Women."

Billy struggled to keep a straight face.

Alan shot Hana an exasperated look. "Would you quit goofing around?" He scowled at Billy. "Listen, Alan and I volunteered for this brain–computer test program and came in yesterday for initial consultations. We both met with some research assistant named Kyle. We're both scheduled to meet a Dr. Blackmore this evening, but we need to speak with Kyle or the doctor right away."

"Ah yes, Dr. Blackmore of MU neuroscience studies," Billy said. "He's an adjunct professor involved in specialized research. I'm not familiar with the program, but I've been away on vacation. So, what's the problem?"

"Yes," Hana said as she turned to Alan. "How would you explain the problem?"

Alan noticed she had a slight grin. It occurred to him that their story was so preposterous, nobody would believe them. People switching minds? Anybody would think a person saying such a thing was delusional.

Instead, Alan sat with his mouth open, lost as to what to say next. Both Hana and Billy looked at him expectantly.

"I ... We ...," he stammered. "We want to talk with Dr. Blackmore."

"He's not here," Billy said. "Is there something wrong?"

"Well ... I ..." Alan remained tongue-tied.

Hana leaned toward Billy and spoke quietly. "Both of us woke up today with our minds transferred to the other's body. Right now I'm Hana, and she's Alan."

There was a moment of silence as Billy and Hana stared at one another. Then Hana straightened up and laughed. Billy smiled. Alan sat there, surprised by the whole thing. Now that she had stated their case aloud, he was more convinced than ever of the craziness of their situation.

"Just kidding, Billy," she said with a smile. "But we really do need to see Dr. Blackmore."

"Give me a second." He stood and left the room.

Alan kept his voice low. "What the hell do you think you're doing? Can't you take this seriously?"

She grinned. "Sorry. I'm enjoying being a man. It's funny to see how people interact with me in a different manner. It's kind of cool, actually."

"Cool?"

"I don't know. I feel like people make assumptions about me because I'm a man. They pay more attention to me. They may even be more respectful."

"No kidding. If one more person ignores me to talk to you,

I'm going to crown them."

"Welcome to my world."

He crossed his arms and scowled. "You're welcome to it. I want to go back to being a guy."

"What? If you can't handle the heat, you should stay out of the kitchen."

"Hey, I didn't ask to be put in the kitchen. Besides, I think the first person I should crown should be *you*."

"What?" She gave a look of mock surprise. "What did I say?"

"'Now, dear'? Really? Is there such a thing as a female chauvinist?"

"Aw, come on. That was funny."

"Between you and me it might be funny, but Billy thinks you two have a certain male camaraderie that involves mocking *me*."

"Gee, aren't *you* touchy. I wonder if it's that time of the month."

He glared at her. "I swear to God I could scream." He leaned closer. "You seem to be enjoying the male experience. Perhaps I could help you get the *full* experience."

She smiled and nodded. "Ooh, that sounds like fun."

"How about I punch you right in the nuts? Trust me — you haven't lived as a man until you've felt the ultimate in male pain. It's an experience you'll never forget." He gave her an evil grin. "I'll be more than happy to oblige whenever you say the word."

"Boy, you can be quite heartless. You'd punch yourself in the balls just to teach me a lesson?"

"It may be my body, but *you'd* be the one feeling the pain. I think that might be a good trade-off."

The door opened, and Billy came back in holding a business card. "Here's Dr. Blackmore's contact information." He handed the card to Hana. Before she could read it, Alan snatched it out of her hand.

"Julian Blackmore, PhD, neuroscience research, Manhattan University School of Medicine." He looked at Billy. "This is his address on campus?"

"Yes," he said, glancing at his watch. "From what I found out, he'll be there this afternoon after one."

Alan sat looking at the card while rubbing his chin.

"What are you thinking?" Hana said.

"What else? We need to visit the good doctor."

"You must be quite concerned about your procedures," Billy said.

Alan glanced up at him. "That's putting it mildly." He got to his feet. "Billy, thanks for your help."

"Glad to be of service. Maybe you can figure out how to get back into your own bodies." He gave them a wry smile.

"Yeah," Alan said. "Yeah, that's it." He gestured toward Hana. "He's always such a wiseguy."

Alan moved toward the door. "Come on, hubby. The good woman has spoken." *Two could play at this game*, he thought.

As Alan stepped into the hall, Hana thanked Billy again before adding in a louder voice, "Coming, dear!"

Chapter 7

"I'm dying here." Hana held her stomach as she walked. "First, you give me tea then you give me a bagel. How about offering me lunch?"

Alan glanced at her but kept walking. "If you were a gentleman, you'd be offering *me* lunch."

She paused. "Oh right — I'm the guy."

"Well, duh. Then again, do I remember I'm the woman?"

"I think you have a way to go."

"What's that supposed to mean?" He looked at her with a raised eyebrow. "I didn't seem to have any trouble attracting the male animal last night."

"Emphasis on *animal.* You seem to forget that after a few drinks — and especially after dark — your average male is running around with enough hormones in his body to light up a ten-story office building."

"Nice image."

"I suppose it was better than saying that most guys would fuck anything that moves."

He rolled his eyes. "Oh, brother."

"What? Are you going to say that's not true?"

"Well, no ... I guess I don't enjoy hearing it said out loud. Under other circumstances, I like to think we guys bring more to the table than an overactive libido."

"Okay, I'll give you that. But don't forget that last night I was dressed to kill, and the weak-willed male couldn't resist my siren call."

"Please — we can't all be that bad."

"No?"

Alan realized she was no longer at his side. He stopped and turned around. She grinned and pointed at him. "I bet I could hook you and reel you in."

He gazed at her — no, at himself, a six-foot man dressed in a suit and tie — and reflected on this reversal of roles. "In light of our current situation, I'd say that's a moot point."

She stepped up to him and put her arm around his

shoulders, leaning in to speak softly in his ear. "Can my female mind seduce your male mind? Of course, with this body switch, you present me with an even greater challenge. Kinky, yes? But I'm willing to give it a go if you are."

He took her arm off his shoulders and pushed her away. "Down, tiger. I have a reputation to protect."

"Really now?" She made a sly face before looking up at an overhead sign. "Hey, let's go in here."

He read *Charlie's Diner* and shrugged. "Sure, why not?"

They went in and sat at a booth. Alan took the menus held up by a sugar container and a bottle of ketchup and passed one to Hana. They were both silent as they perused the offerings.

A waitress wandered over to their table. "Good morning," she said, laying out two paper placemats and bundles of silverware before them. "What can I get you folks today?"

Hana studied the menu, and without looking up said, "I'll get the chicken Caesar salad and the lady will have—"

Alan kicked her under the table. "I'll have the hamburger and fries. May I get a cup of coffee to start? With milk?"

Hana shot him a dirty look. "Could I get tea?"

The waitress wrote on a pad. "Got it. I'll be back in a moment with your drinks."

Hana leaned across the table and whispered, "What the heck do you think you're doing to my figure?"

"What?"

"A hamburger and fries?"

"I'm hungry." He gave her a mocking look. "You should work out."

"I don't think I'm bad."

"It all adds up over time, whether we realize it or not."

"Okay, Mr. Bigshot Six-Pack Abs."

"So glad you noticed. I've busted my butt enough at the gym to get them."

"You've got yourself a decent body."

"Just decent?"

"*I'd* sleep with you."

Alan smiled dryly. "High praise, indeed."

"Actually, it is. I could show you a good time."

"I'm sure you could." He paused. "You seem to enjoy your work."

"You mean I enjoy sex?"

"Well, that's what I was saying."

"Who doesn't?"

"Let's just say the majority of people are not so overt about sex in their conversations."

Hana shrugged. "Too bad for them. Life would be so much better if everybody was less hung up and more demonstrative about this intimate part of their lives. It's not bad, it's *good*. It's not embarrassing, it's *liberating*."

The waitress set down the cups and a teapot.

"Thank you," Alan said. He turned back to Hana. "There's Hana the philosopher again."

"I guess I do, from time to time, reflect on the human condition. Wouldn't *you* like to make the world a better place?"

"Sure. I guess I hadn't considered doing so through sex."

"Why not? Change the world one person at a time." She tapped her chin thoughtfully. "Well, not *always* one person at a time," she chortled.

"You're quite the bubbly personality."

"I'm not here for a long time. I'm here for a good time."

"Good philosophy. So tell me, how did you become a pros — an escort?"

She grinned. "Prostitute. You can say it. I'm not offended. The term 'sex worker' is preferable, but I've accepted — or tried to accept — that some people look down on me for what I do."

"How did you get into such a line of work?"

"I'm not a druggie. I don't come from a broken home. I'm pretty much your girl next door with a university degree. I speak French fluently and enough Spanish to get by. I've traveled and seen a bit of the world. But in among that, I do like sex. And I discovered I enjoy pleasing people. And pleasuring them. It may be hard to understand, hard for a man, but there *is* a certain thrill to being a conduit of pleasure."

"Conduit of pleasure?"

"Yes — I'm the means by which someone else attains pleasure. I'm their instrument of lust."

"Isn't that objectifying yourself?"

Hana tilted her head and pursed her lips. "Aren't we all objects of desire? To someone else, I mean. But as a woman, I *experience* that a man wants me. He desires me, even craves me. He's incomplete without me, and it's only with me he can achieve that which he seeks."

"Which is?"

"The obvious is sex. We don't seem to realize that the primordial urge to copulate is built into our DNA. I would argue that it's a physical need, as much as breathing or eating."

"Isn't that stretching things a bit?" Alan smiled wryly. "You're not going to die if you don't have sex, but you can't go without air or food."

"True. I'm not going to die if I don't have chocolate chip cookie dough ice cream, but that doesn't mean it isn't desirable in my life and that I wouldn't actively seek it. The problem is that our society frowns on pleasure, especially sexual pleasure. We've linked sex to traditional constructs like marriage and defined it as occurring only between a married man and woman, strictly for procreation. Anything else is verboten. We completely ignore sex as a fundamental right of every individual, and we ignore it as a physical need."

"Where are you going with this?"

"Do you masturbate?" She looked at him with a hint of a smile.

He hesitated. "Well, yes."

"Why?"

"Uh ... because it feels good."

"Anything wrong with that?"

He shrugged. "I guess not."

"So what if *I* masturbated you?"

"I suppose that would be nice."

"What if I did it for money?"

"Well, uh, I could be arrested."

"Why? What business is it of anybody what you and I do together? If I agree to go home with you and have sex, nobody says anything. However, if I agree to go home with you and have sex but ask you to give me money, it's a crime. How odd. My body for free is okay, but putting a value on my body is an offense. In both cases, the sex is consensual. In both cases, it involves a mutual agreement between two people."

"Isn't selling yourself for sex degrading?"

"Pardon me, but what the hell? You're setting my worth as a human being, as a woman, according to whether or not I have sex. If I'm chaste, I'm valuable. If I'm no longer a virgin, I'm no longer valuable. This is the age-old view of women as chattel. I'm not a human being, I'm a piece of property. I'll take a pass, thank you very much."

She played with her fork. "I can provide you with a number of services designed to make you feel better and charge you money, all within the bounds of the law. However, I can't do anything sexual with you — which I would argue also makes you feel better — and charge you money. There's a contradiction there."

"What about exploitation? What about sex trafficking?"

"Why is it that people jump up and down about the exploitation of human beings when it comes to sex but ignore the same exploitation elsewhere in our society? Women are treated unfairly in the workplace. They can do exactly the same job as a male counterpart, but because of the very fact that they're female, they get less money. *That's* exploitation. People working in service industries like fast food make less than minimum wage. *That's* exploitation. Immigrant workers sometimes slave for a mere pittance but can do nothing about their plight out of fear of getting deported. *That's* exploitation."

As Hana continued her tirade, Alan glanced around the diner. No one seemed to be paying them any attention. He returned his focus on her as his stomach grumbled.

"Sex?" she said. "You're worried about sex? Don't make me laugh! You ignore the daily exploitation of millions of people around the globe for everything other than sex. I would add that for some odd reason, people equate sex work with slavery. You *hire* a sex worker; you don't *buy* them. Just like you hire a plumber, you don't buy them. The idea of ownership and sex is part of the traditionalist patriarchy, and we need to move away from the past. Sex work isn't slavery any more than any type of voluntary work is slavery."

Alan tipped his head to one side and gazed at her. "You've put a lot of thought into this."

"The average person is ignorant of what goes on in the world. People jump up and down about the latest issue they see on television, but don't know what's going on next door. We have no idea how the world works, how it *truly* works."

The waitress arrived and set down two plates. "Chicken Caesar. Hamburger and fries."

"Ooh, that looks good," Hana said. "But I have to visit the little boys' room. I'll be right back." She got up and went to the back of the restaurant.

Alan picked up the ketchup bottle and, holding it upside down, slapped the bottom. Satisfied with the quantity on his plate, he picked up a french fry, dipped it in the ketchup, and plopped it in his mouth.

"Alan!" Hana's voice from the back sounded panicky. "Alan!"

He jumped up, took several paces in the direction of the restrooms, then hurried back and picked up his purse. Dashing toward her continued cries, he found the men's room door slightly ajar. He pushed it open and said, "What's the prob—"

"Get it out! Get it out!" She stood in the middle of the room flailing her arms. "It's caught in the zipper!"

He looked down to see her penis — *his* penis — sticking out of her pants. "Hold still."

Alan dropped to his knees and held the penis to the side as he inspected the situation. "Okay. I don't want you to move."

"Is this going to hurt?" Hana sounded alarmed.

"No." He let go of the penis and used both hands to seize one edge of the zipper and bend it to expand the distance between the teeth. Still holding the zipper, he raised an index finger and gently pushed the skin out from between the pieces of metal.

"Ow! Ow! Ow!" She looked at him, panic-stricken.

There was a loud squeak as the door to the men's room swung open. They both turned. A man took a step into the room and froze. He looked down at Alan, looked up at Hana, and looked again at Alan. Wide-eyed, he mumbled an apology then immediately spun on his foot and left. The door squeaked shut.

"There. You're free." Alan let go of the zipper and stood back up.

"Jesus Christ, that hurt." Hana grabbed a hold of her penis and turned it back and forth, examining the skin. "How the hell does skin get caught in a zipper? Does that happen often?"

He shrugged. "Hasn't everybody got something caught in a zipper? But yes, probably all guys at one time or another have had to deal with this. You learn to pay attention."

"Oh my God, I'm going to have castration nightmares!"

"Make sure you hold onto yourself and keep the skin away from the zipper teeth."

She finished up, and they returned to their table.

"I hope to God that never happens to me again." She sat down and looked at her plate. "Whew! I'm hungry."

"Me too."

As they started in on their lunches, Alan's thoughts strayed again to their previous conversation and Hana's passionate defense of the exploited. "I can picture you out on the street marching for social change," he said.

"I'm never going to be Gandhi or Martin Luther King, Jr., but I try to do my part. There's a lot of screwed up things in the world and we should all do our part."

"Including sex?"

"Yes, including sex. Listen, I'm sure you disapprove of me, but I'm comfortable with myself and what I do. I've met some wonderful people, and I've had some wonderful experiences outside of what you would call normal society. I refuse to let a puritanical culture with its patriarchal traditions dictate how I should live my life. There's far more to life than a monogamous marriage in a suburban home with a white picket fence and two-point-five children."

"So what is it that you seek outside the confines of what one may think of as the norm?"

"What is it that *anyone's* looking for when partnering with somebody?"

He shrugged.

"That connection with another soul," she said. "We're born alone, and we die alone. In between, we spend a lot of time trying not to be alone. Sex is a gift from God: our way of not being alone."

"What is it that you see in sex?"

"Wholeness. Yin and yang. Synergy. The whole is greater than the sum of its parts." She took a sip of her tea. "Sex is good, but there's a special time just after sex when two human beings experience an almost spiritual closeness to one another. It's a magical moment, and probably the closest anyone will ever get to merging with someone else into a single mind, a single spirit. It's two people as one."

"You paint a beautiful portrait of nirvana, or whatever you want to call it. Unfortunately, real life doesn't always seem to be as wonderful as you describe it."

"Of course not. We live in a funny society. Women learn to suppress their sexuality, and men learn to suppress their *sens*uality. Sex is bad. Sex is to be avoided. And yet we can't escape our physical desires. We remain conflicted by our needs and by our religious upbringing, in which pleasure is not considered good."

"What are we missing?" Alan picked up another french fry as he watched her.

"Openness. Honesty. And more importantly, compersion."

"Compersion? What's that?"

Hana looked away as she mulled over his question. "It's when you feel good about somebody else's happiness. But when I say happiness ..."

"Yes?"

"I could be talking about a situation in which your partner has a romantic or sexual relationship with somebody else."

Alan's jaw dropped. "What?"

"Think about it. Compersion is the opposite of jealousy. If you truly wanted your partner to be happy, would you stop them from doing what they want? Would you stop them from being with whoever they want to be with?"

He frowned. "This is getting weird."

"You're being a traditionalist. You've been brainwashed to think monogamy is the only acceptable form of relationship."

"So, you think we can all run around having sex with anybody?"

"See? Hyperbole! You immediately jump to the far end of the spectrum. If it isn't white, it's black. There's no such thing as gray." She reached across the table and took a french fry from his plate, then contemplated him as she chewed.

"Well, I ..." Alan faltered, creasing his brow.

"Do you have lunch with every person you meet?"

"Uh, no."

"Why not?"

"I guess I don't have the time or, more importantly, I'm not interested in every person I meet."

"So apply that to sex. You wouldn't have sex with everybody you meet because you don't necessarily *like* everybody."

He hesitated. "I suppose."

"Of course. Sometimes lunch is just lunch. It doesn't lead to dinner. It certainly doesn't lead to a long-term relationship. It's just lunch. But during that hour you're together, it can be an enjoyable experience. It can be open and honest with a remarkable degree of intimacy and closeness, all without you having to exchange marriage vows and commit for the rest of your life."

"I guess."

The waitress set down their bill. Hana looked at it.

"I'll take care of it," Alan said. "I may no longer have my body, but I still have my knowledge, and I know the PIN for my credit card and can sign."

She grinned. "Oh? Should I be a gentleman and pick up the tab?"

"Would your chivalry be lost on me? I'm not sure I could get used to men being polite to me any more than I could get used to men hitting on me."

"Hey, you have a unique opportunity! Heck, *I* have a unique opportunity. How many people get to try out the other side of the sexual divide?"

"Unique opportunity? I think I'd prefer to have my own body back."

At the cashier's station, Alan presented his credit card. As he handed the terminal back, he noticed the man from the restroom staring at them from a nearby booth.

The waitress handed him the receipt, which he folded and put in his purse. As he turned to the door, he saw that the man was still staring at him. "Look, man," Alan said, "it's no big deal." He pointed to Hana. "She got her penis caught in her zipper, and I was merely trying to help."

"*She?*" Hana grabbed his arm and directed him toward the door. "Let's get out of here and find Dr. Blackmore."

Chapter 8

Alan and Hana had to ask several people for directions to Dr. Blackmore's office, curiously not housed in the Center for Neural Science. It was almost as though nobody knew of the doctor. While the business card Billy had given them seemed legitimate, Blackmore didn't appear to be well known. Alan and Hana had expected BCI research to be more visible on campus.

Eventually, they were directed to a nondescript two-story structure labeled *Building 42*, hidden behind several larger department buildings. They stepped through the doorway and found themselves on a small landing, with stairs leading down to the basement and up to what seemed to be a reception area. They climbed the stairs and looked around. Nobody was in sight.

Hana whispered, "Is anybody here?"

"Beats me," Alan said.

Just then, Alan noticed a black button on the wall above a sign that read, *Press here for service*. He peeked around one more time and pushed the button. Somewhere in the building a buzzer sounded. They stood there, waiting. The building seemed perfectly quiet, but Alan thought there might be the sound of machines or muffled activity elsewhere.

After a few moments footsteps sounded on a hard tile floor, getting louder as they got closer. A door to one side burst open, and a bearded man in a lab coat stepped onto the landing.

"Yes?" The man eyed them curiously.

"Are you Dr. Blackmore?" Alan said.

"Ah, you must be Mr. and Mrs. Maitland."

Alan sighed. "We're not married."

"Whatever," Blackmore said. The doctor walked up to Alan and peered at his face.

"Wait," Alan said. "How do you know us?"

"Billy phoned to tell me you were coming over. You're the two my research student set up yesterday with our portable scanner." Blackmore moved to Hana and examined her. "Anything you want to tell me? I can't tell."

"Can't tell what?" she said.

He walked around her studying the back of her neck. He ran his index finger over the hollow at the top of her spine, just under the skull, and she flinched.

Alan watched, uneasy. "What are you doing, Doctor?"

"Just feeling where the neural implant is located. I don't see anything wrong, so what's the problem?"

"Problem? Doctor, I think you have a really, really *big* problem." Alan's voice echoed in the space. "What the heck is this thing, anyway?"

"We've been doing research into various aspects of neuroscience, studying the brain in an attempt to shed light on the mechanisms by which we think."

Alan listened intently.

"A great deal of the research has focused on deciphering what amounts to an organic computer. The term *computer* seems to be inadequate to describe the complexity of a system that can think, create, dream, and remember. The processing power inside the human head is without parallel in technology.

"Recent breakthroughs in neural linkages have opened doors to the brain, providing never-before-seen access to the mind. These new developments have opened our eyes to the possibility of direct links between human brains and computers, synergistic intelligence, and especially artificial telepathy — that is, direct brain-to-brain connections. It's all in its infancy, but what we've seen so far has excited the scientific community."

Blackmore paused to catch his breath. "As a first step in our explorations of this relatively new field of study, we developed a subcutaneous chip that provides a remote neural link to an individual's cerebral functions. We can tap into a person's head and with a wifi connection, we can link their brain to a computer to transfer information. That information can then be interpreted as commands so a user can operate devices using only their thoughts — anything from an artificial limb to a machine, even a car."

"I'm assuming," Alan said, "that this is a two-way connection. The implant not only sends information, it can receive it."

"Yes. The computer sends information back to the brain, but how that information is interpreted by the brain is still under study. In theory, the information can be anything from the results of a Google search to the images from a video camera or the sensory input of an artificial hand touching something. The computer and its associated devices could become an extension of the brain itself."

"Listen carefully to what I'm going to say." Alan took a deep breath. "Hana and I have no idea what happened or how any of this is possible, but our minds have been switched."

Both of them looked at Blackmore expectantly, but Blackmore simply stared at Alan.

"Dr. Blackmore, did you hear me?"

The doctor blinked several times and opened his mouth to speak, but said nothing. "I heard you. But it doesn't seem to register."

Alan pointed to Hana. "That body is Alan Maitland." He pointed to himself. "This body is Hana Toussaint." He pointed to Hana's head. "That mind is Hana Toussaint." He pointed to his own. "This mind is Alan Maitland."

"What in blue blazes are you talking about?"

"Doctor, our minds have been switched. I'm not Hana — I'm Alan. My mind, the mind of Alan Maitland, is in the body of Hana Toussaint."

"That's not possible!"

"Not possible? Doctor, I assure you, it *is* possible. I'm living proof it's possible. We — both Hana and I — are examples of this possibility. The question is, what are you going to do about it?"

Blackmore smiled wryly. "This is a joke. You're trying to pull one over on me. Is the chancellor in on this? He's always giving me a hard time about funding, saying we're doing work that would be better suited to a science fiction movie than real life. That man is no visionary when it comes to the future!"

Hana stepped closer. "Doctor, Alan isn't joking. I'm not Alan — I'm Hana. My brain, my mind, is now housed in this body."

Blackmore chuckled. "Okay, I can go along with a gag. Let's take you downstairs and give you each a scan. I have your cerebral signatures on file and can conclusively prove who you are."

The doctor turned and walked toward the stairs. Hana and Alan looked at each other warily and followed.

"The chancellor has it in for me," Blackmore said. "Sooner or later, I think he's going to convince the Board of Regents that this school can do without my specialized research. After all, what school thinks it will attract serious students if a member of the staff is doing stuff out of *Star Wars* or *The Matrix*? Where's the practical application in everyday life when students want an education that will give them a job?"

At the bottom of the stairs, Blackmore turned right and headed down a hall that seemed to run the length of the building. About halfway along the passage, he opened a door and led them into a laboratory. "Okay, Mr. and Mrs. Jokester. Let's prove who you really are."

He nodded to Alan and gestured toward a chair situated beside a complex computer system with a large monitor. "Hana, have a seat." He paused looking thoughtful. "Wait." He pointed to Hana and said, "Sorry. Hana, would you care to sit down?" He again gestured to the chair. "Or Alan. Whatever."

Blackmore picked up a helmet speckled with wired attachments that led to a junction box beside the computer. As he adjusted it on Hana's head, he said, "I'm going to make a scan of your brain." He pressed the power button on the scanner, and a buzzing noise started. He clicked through several menus on the computer. "One sec." In the middle of the screen, a bar moved from zero percent to one hundred. "Done."

Blackmore took the helmet off her head. "Your turn, Alan."

He took her place, and the doctor secured the helmet on him.

Once again, Blackmore fiddled with the controls as he watched the monitor. "Finished." He removed the helmet and returned to the computer. "I'm calling up your previous signatures so we can see them side by side."

Hana and Alan crowded around the console and peeked over Blackmore's shoulders. He loaded the scans and arranged them on the screen beside each other. Labels at the bottom of the panels identified them as *Alan-original*, *Hana-original*, *Alan-now*, and *Hana-now*. Alan studied the squiggles, not understanding what he was viewing.

"The machine has functions that allow me to compare your signatures," Blackmore said. "I can have it delve into the minutiae of the scans and accurately compare the graphs."

He clicked the mouse a few times and bars appeared over each graph. "The bars represent the averages of the various highs and lows." He held a hand up to the top left panel, labeled *Alan-original*, and pointed with the other hand to the *Alan-now* panel. He looked back and forth between the two graphs as he traced his fingers along the bars.

"That's odd."

"What?" Alan said.

"They don't match."

Blackmore took his hand from *Alan-now* and moved it down to *Hana-now*. He compared *Alan-original* to *Hana-now* before switching to Hana's graphs and performing the same exercise. Then he dropped his hands and stared at the screen. "This isn't possible."

Alan said, "What's your machine telling you?"

"Just a second." The doctor went through the comparisons a second time. "I don't believe this."

"Well, Dr. Blackmore, do you believe us now?" Hana said.

He sat gazing into space, then got up and paced the room. He stared at the floor, concentrating. He scratched his head. "I'm perplexed. I see the graphs and I've done the comparisons, but it doesn't make any sense. How is this even remotely possible?"

"Doctor," Alan said, "you said these implants can both send and receive information."

Blackmore stopped. "Yes."

"What happens if the device receives information?"

"It passes it on to the brain. However, the user must learn to interpret the incoming electrical signals. After all, a video camera is not the same as a human eye and the sensory input of an artificial hand is not the same as one's own touch. I've done this myself, and I admit it takes some getting used to."

"Tell us more about this implant process."

"First, we do a complete scan of a person's head. This bioelectrical recording is a snapshot of the brain's activity, representing its current thoughts and memories. The information gets transferred to an implant chip, and that chip is inserted under the skin. From there, a wireless link is set up with a remote computer, and a neural connection is established between the computer and the person."

Alan knitted his brow. "What's the purpose of recording a person's brain scan then transferring it to the implant chip?"

"A neural link is personalized to an individual. To function, to act as a bridge between the person and the computer, the chip must first be seeded with complete information about the host brain. One day somebody will develop something generic, but the current state of technology demands this personalization of the chip or it won't work."

Alan remained quiet, rubbing his chin. Hana kept looking back and forth between Alan and Blackmore.

"So," Alan said, "you do a full scan on an individual. You have this scan recorded. Then you transfer the recording to a chip, and you insert that chip into the person."

"Yes."

Alan kept rubbing his chin and glanced toward the ceiling. "Doctor?"

"Yes?"

"What would happen if you put Hana's chip in me and my chip in Hana?"

"The communication link between the brain and the chip wouldn't work."

Alan watched Blackmore as he sat looking down at the floor, turning absentmindedly on the swivel chair. He put one hand on the edge of the console and tapped a finger.

Finally, the doctor stood and walked to a side table. He picked up a small device and came back to Alan. "Turn around," he said.

Alan showed his back to the doctor. Blackmore adjusted the controls on the device and held it against the back of Alan's neck. Studying the read-out on the device, he pursed his lips but said nothing.

Then Blackmore walked to Hana and went through the same procedure. When he finished, he sat back down on the swivel chair and continued to tap a finger on the edge of the console.

"I guess from your puzzled look that something has gone amiss," Alan said.

Hana looked at the doctor. "Is it true?"

Blackmore slumped in the chair, defeated. "Yes, it's true."

"So, let me recap," Alan said. "You scan my brain, record it, and put it on a chip. You then put that chip into Hana's head, and, for whatever reason, the recording of my brain overwrites her brain, thus turning Hana into me."

Blackmore nodded. "The recording seems to have rewired the synapses of the brain with the bioelectrical signature of another brain, changing the thought patterns and memories to those of the recorded brain."

Alan raised an eyebrow. "How do you put it back?"

Blackmore faced him. "I have no idea how this could have happened in the first place. I can't reverse this if I don't even know what it is. Heck, as far as I know, this could be permanent."

Hana smiled as she ran a hand down her chest. "I suppose there are worse fates."

Alan glared at her. "I want my body back."

She shrugged. "Finders keepers."

"Not funny." Alan regarded Blackmore. "If something made this happen, I'm assuming something can undo it."

"That would seem a reasonable assumption." Blackmore shook his head. "But ..."

"But what?" Alan said.

"I've never seen it happen before. I've tried the chip. I've had several members of staff and students participate in trials, and nobody has ever reported such a phenomenon."

"Have you ever put a chip in the wrong person?"

"No, I haven't—" The doctor froze, puzzlement etched on his face. He then looked at Alan. Alan looked back at him. They both said at the same time: "Kyle."

"This still doesn't make any sense." Blackmore scrunched up his face. "In all our tests, the brain scan on the chip had to match the host brain, or the communication link between chip and brain would fail. Nobody's ever seen what you're experiencing. Who would have thought the consciousness of one person could be transferred to another?"

"Who would have thought? Who would have thought?" Alan paced the room. "What the hell are we going to do?"

"I can stick the right chips back in the right heads, but I have no reason to believe from anything I've done up to this point that it would do any good. This never should have happened." The doctor wiped a bead of sweat from his brow.

Alan stopped and stared at each of them in turn, disbelieving. "What if I have to spend the rest of my life like this?" He threw his arms up and paced again. "Fuck!"

The doctor glanced at him with a pleading look. "I'm under a lot of pressure to succeed. The chancellor is constantly on my back, and there's always the threat of my funding getting cut. If I don't produce something tangible, a meaningful success in the real world, I could find my entire research lab shut down and all of us out of work. Now this? If word of your problem gets out, there's no doubt I'm in big trouble." Blackmore wiped his brow. "I'm sorry. We've worked very hard to perfect our work. We double-checked — no, *triple-*checked — our work, and were sure we had covered any eventuality. Our recent success led us to believe we had cleared all obstacles, but this problem could end up being a major setback for the program."

Alan grimaced. "Dr. Blackmore, I've been involved in project management for years. If there's one mistake I've seen repeatedly, it's overconfidence. You said you triple-checked everything. You didn't *quadruple*-check. Your guy mixed up the chips. Your guy put the *wrong chips* in our heads. You had no procedure in place to do a last-minute verification to ensure a proper match between the person and the chip. This reminds me of stories in which a surgeon amputates the wrong leg."

The doctor's shoulders sagged. "I'm so sorry. I had no idea things could go so horribly wrong."

Alan stopped his tirade. "I want coffee." He faced Hana and the doctor. "Let's get some caffeine and think this through. I want to give up being a woman and get back to being a man."

"Get back to wearing the pants, not the panties, in the family," Hana added dryly.

Alan ignored her.

Chapter 9

"I propose that the two of you come back to the lab tomorrow morning at ten." Blackmore said. "I'm going to rerun scans of your brains, reseed the chips, and see if I can recreate the circumstances of your transfer."

"A quadruple-check, Doctor." Alan's voice quivered as he sought to control his temper.

"Yes. A quadruple-check."

Alan wanted to solicit the doctor's cooperation. He wanted to encourage his sense of guilt over the screw-up and inspire him to do whatever necessary to undo his mistake. So far, he sensed, Blackmore seemed determined to make amends, get it right, and get them back into their proper bodies. "Let's do it," Alan said.

The three of them stood and left the coffee shop.

Alan waved. "Until tomorrow morning, Doctor."

"Yes." Blackmore headed off across the campus.

"Should I slap him silly?" Alan stared after the doctor. "Or do I accept that this problem is beyond his control? Was our situation preventable or was it inevitable?"

Blackmore disappeared around the corner of a building.

"On the one hand, I'm angry," continued Alan, letting out a big sigh. "On the other, I feel dejected by the possibility I may not get out of this situation." He shook his head. "Oh God. What a mess!"

Hana put a hand on his shoulder. "I'm sure it's going to work out."

The two of them stood for a moment, saying nothing.

"Why don't you come back to my place?" Alan said.

"Oh?" She feigned surprise. "Are you asking me to spend the night? What kind of guy do you think I am?"

"Oh, brother." He didn't hide his annoyance. "I merely thought that neither of us has any place to go under the present circumstances. If we stay together, we could go back to the lab together in the morning. Besides, I have two bedrooms and you don't. I'd prefer not to sleep on the couch."

"Always practical. So much for romance." She smiled. "Why don't we drop back by my place and pick you up a few things? You can't go around wearing the same clothes."

As they walked up Hana's street, they once again found the super out on the steps of her building. This time, he sat watching the street.

"Hi, Harvey," Alan said.

"Hello, Hana." Harvey nodded to Hana and said, "Alan."

Hana nodded back but didn't say anything.

"Oh, Hana?"

Both Hana and Alan said, "Yes?"

Harvey gave them a curious look.

"Sorry," Hana said.

Harvey continued, seemingly nonplussed. "If Marvin drops around again, what do you want me to do?"

Alan looked at Hana, then back at Harvey. "Well ..."

"Let him in," Hana said. "We do business together, but he's more than just an acquaintance."

"Yes," Alan said. "Business."

Harvey smiled good-naturedly. "You're nearly finishing each other's sentences. It's almost like you're married."

Hana chuckled. "Yeah." She took Alan's arm and led him to the door.

"Have a good one." Harvey went back to watching the street.

As they climbed the stairs, she said, "Harvey's a nice man. His wife died a couple of years ago, just a month after his retirement. They'd made plans to do some traveling, but then she got the cancer diagnosis and was dead within six months. Harvey didn't know what to do with himself, so he took on this position. He told me it gives him extra cash and keeps him occupied."

Hana packed a bag with things for Alan, including feminine products and a change of clothes. It was late afternoon by the time they returned to his condo. Alan poured two glasses of wine and led Hana out onto the balcony.

"A balcony like this, recessed into the building instead of

sticking out from it, is called a loggia. I can stand out here even when it's raining. It's enjoyable."

"Nice," she said.

They leaned on the railing and gazed out over the cityscape.

"You're living on top of the world," remarked Hana.

"It's taken a lot of hard work to get here. But, admittedly, there was a lot of luck involved too."

"Really?"

"I've never forgotten what my dad told me: you can work hard and still lose. Good people work very, very hard to win, but at the end of the day, there's only one winner. Working hard gets you into the race. Sometimes a little luck means you win."

"So, now what?"

"What do you mean?" he said.

"You work hard. You win. You reach the peak of success. Now what?"

Alan chuckled. "Good question."

"More wins? More stuff? Success times two?"

"There has to be an end to that sometime. How much stuff can a person have?"

"You tell me," Hana said. "I sometimes think men have a tendency to push for success, then more and more success, without stopping to smell the roses."

"That's possible. We should try to find balance in life."

"And where does Mr. Alan Maitland find balance?"

He reflected awhile, then said, "Origami."

"Origami?"

"It's the traditional Japanese art of paper folding."

"I know what it is. You fold paper in your spare time?"

"Well," he said. "No."

"Ah, I see. Forever evasive." Hana took a sip of her wine and contemplated the skyline, filled with streaks of light from the setting sun. "There's no Mrs. Maitland and there's no girlfriend."

"Nope."

"Are you sure you're not gay?"

He laughed. "Forever blunt and direct."

"Why waste time? Life is uncertain. Eat dessert first."

He looked out. "Yes, I suppose ..."

She leaned over, tilted her head, and kissed him full on the lips.

He jumped and backed up a step. "Jesus. What the hell are you trying to do?"

She grinned at him.

He stared at her, miffed, then relaxed and smiled. "Oh, I get it. You love to jerk my chain. You want to provoke something."

"I said this was a unique opportunity. Tomorrow we may be back to normal, and all of this will be over. Wouldn't it be a shame to pass up this chance?"

"Chance for what?"

"There's an old saying: I'd rather regret the things I've done than regret the things I haven't done."

He shook his head. "No way."

"Way."

"Forget it."

"Twenty years from now, you're going to be sitting around wondering. And regretting."

"I'll take that chance."

"I jerked off this morning," she said.

He gaped at her. "You did *what?*"

"You heard me."

He held a hand to his forehead and groaned. "Oh my God."

"What? I've given a few handjobs over the years. I just had to try it on myself."

"And ...?"

"And what?"

"How was it abusing my body?"

"Pretty good, actually. You're very responsive."

"What does that mean?"

"You respond very well to stimulation. Of course, I do add to the mix an excellent ability to focus on the matter at hand."

"You're incorrigible." He tried not to smile.

"Hey, I know what I like." She took another sip of wine. "Haven't you given my old bod a whirl?"

He whipped around. "No!"

"Why not? Opportunity's knocking."

"I ... Well ..."

"If you want, I can help."

He sipped his wine and looked at her over the rim of the glass.

"Listen, you," she said. "You're among friends. We have no secrets. You're never going to be closer to another human being in your life, so there's no need to be embarrassed. There's nothing to be gained by holding back. I don't judge you. I *accept* you. You're free to say or do anything you want. I know that body inside and out, and I would be more than happy to show you how to take the old girl out for a spin. I guarantee you would thoroughly enjoy yourself."

"I don't know what to say. I feel uncomfortable, and I can't help feeling that anything I say will just encourage you. You're liberated and I'm reserved. I don't see that changing anytime soon." He gulped down the last of his drink and said, "I need more wine."

As he stepped inside, the phone rang. The call display showed the concierge's desk and Alan hesitated, remembering that his voice was no longer *his* voice. But thinking he could improvise, he picked up the receiver. "Hello?"

"Good evening. This is André at security. Is Mr. Maitland available?"

"Uh, he's tied up right now. May I take a message?"

"There's a Jack Morley here asking to come up. He says he needs Mr. Maitland's signature."

"Signature?" Alan could hear some muffled voices.

"Something about the Berkshire deal," André said.

He held his hand over the receiver and said, "Oh crap." He called out, "Hana! Come here. Quick!"

She came running. "What's the matter?"

"There's a colleague from work downstairs and he needs to

come up and get my signature. I have to authorize a transaction, and it has to be done today."

"Okay."

"He's the guy I told this morning that I wasn't coming in because I was sick."

"You aren't allowed to skip work because of your period?"

"Shut up. This is serious," Alan said.

"Okay, okay. I'll pretend to be under the weather. You're here to help me — we can make excuses. I'll say I'm feeling better, and we're going out for a private dinner."

"Who am I supposed to be?"

"An old friend who costs two thousand dollars for the evening."

"What? You say something like that and I'll hurt you."

"I'm going to put on a cup."

He groaned. "Oh God, you're going to be the death of me." Alan took his hand off the receiver. "Hello, André? Mr. Maitland says to send him up. Thank you." He hung up and shut his eyes. "I feel a headache coming on."

"If we throw in an extra grand, you should do us both." She tittered.

He strolled to the door, shaking his head, and moaned. "I'm doomed."

Chapter 10

Alan opened the door and held it ajar, waiting. The elevator bell chimed and he heard muffled footsteps on the carpet. He pulled the door open wider as a figure approached.

Jack stood there, eyeing him up and down. "Oh, hello," he said.

Alan held out his hand. "Hana Toussaint. Come on in."

A bellowing voice came from behind him. "Hey, Jack! Come in and get infected."

Alan turned to see Hana wearing a bathrobe and holding a tissue. She coughed and blew her nose. "I think it all caught up with me."

Jack gave her a skeptical look. "You really are sick?"

"It happens to the best of us." She coughed again and wiped her nose. "So, what's up?"

Jack took a couple of steps into the condo and Alan shut the door.

"You were supposed to sign the Berkshire agreement today."

"It couldn't wait? You could have emailed me."

"We have to submit the signed document by six o'clock California time," he said. "A few of us were going out for a bite and—"

"You wanted to check to see if I was lying or not."

"Well ..." Jack smiled slyly.

"Come on in." Hana walked into the main room and sat down in an armchair.

Jack glanced at Alan before following.

"So," Hana said, "did I miss anything important today?" She touched the tissue to her nose.

"Nope. Everything's going okay."

Alan walked around to take a chair beside Hana. He wondered where this was going and wanted to get Jack out of there as quickly as possible.

"Who all is going out?" Hana asked.

"Murphy, Fred, and me. There's a new pub near the office,

and they're having a special on wings tonight."

"Sounds good."

"Murphy, that hound dog, really wanted to go because they're advertising two free drinks for the ladies."

"He'll be the first to get married, settle down, and never look at another woman again."

"Yeah." Jack nodded.

Alan looked between Hana and Jack. Was Jack going to find Hana odd? So far, she seemed to be pulling off this ruse.

Hana held out her hand. "Let's see the document."

"Sure." Jack took out a paper from a suit pocket, unfolded it, and passed it over.

"Got a pen?"

Jack handed one to her.

Hana picked up a book from the coffee table and laid the document on top. "Did you ever see the abstract piece?"

"What?"

Hana pointed behind Jack. "On the wall behind you. I find the geometry of the various cubes to be quite interesting."

Jack turned around and stared at the picture.

"Look carefully," Hana said. "I get the impression I can see other things if I stare at it long enough."

Alan grinned and took the pen from Hana to sign the document.

"Yes," Jack said. "Interesting." He turned back to face them.

Hana put down the book and handed the paper back.

"By the way ..." Jack folded the paper and replaced it put it back in his suit pocket. "Did you finish your projection on prime for the next twelve months? Fagler asked about it, and I was curious to see what you'd come up with. The pundits are conflicted on which way things are going."

Hana hesitated, but Alan put a hand on her arm. "I thought you said it would remain fairly stable for the next twelve months."

She nodded. "Yes, that's right."

Jack regarded Alan. "Ms. Toussaint, are you a student of

the economy?"

He smiled. "Call me Hana. Let's say I dabble. It pays to know what's going on in our world."

Jack nodded. "If I'm not being too forward, what is it that you do, Hana?"

Alan hesitated.

"She's in customer relations, Jack," Hana said. "She's an independent contractor."

"Oh?"

"Yes. She works with some important people downtown."

"Really."

"Yes."

"Anybody I would know?"

Hana smiled at Alan. "Her work is behind the scenes. Due to client confidentiality, she can't say much, but she's very skilled at her job. The clients just keep coming."

Alan gave her arm a harder than normal swat with the back of his hand. "Please, you're embarrassing me."

Hana smiled again. "I know it's hard for you to swallow, but you're doing okay."

Alan opened his mouth to say something, thought better of it, and grabbed hold of the armrests. God, he was going to kill her.

Jack looked back at Hana. "Gee, Alan, you never mentioned anything about your friend. Have you two just recently met?"

"Yes." She put her hand on top of Alan's. "Yesterday, as a matter of fact."

Alan glared at her and gritted his teeth.

"We hit it off," she continued, "and thought we'd see where this may lead." Hana patted his hand and leaned toward him. She spoke quietly, but loud enough for Jack to hear. "What do you think? Seem like a good idea?" She paused, waiting for a reaction. Alan said nothing.

Jack looked at each of them curiously then peeked at his watch. "Oops, gotta go. I said I'd stop by and see what you were up to then meet the guys in twenty minutes. I think my time is up." He stood. "Hana, it was nice meeting you."

Hana and Alan got up.

"Thank you," Alan said, shaking hands with Jack.

"I hope you're feeling better, Alan," Jack said.

Hana moved beside Alan and put an arm around his shoulders. "I have a terrific nurse, Jack. I'm sure she'll give me a hand and I'll be back on top in no time."

Alan gave a forced smile.

He saw Jack out and locked the door, scowling. "You're an idiot!" he snarled as he stomped off to the bathroom.

"What?" She grinned after him.

Alan returned still scowling. "I'll cook dinner."

"A man who can cook!" she said.

"Don't get the wrong impression. My culinary skills are more utilitarian than artistic, but at least I won't poison you."

"Can anyone ask for anything more than to get up from the table knowing they'll live to see the morning?"

"It's only spaghetti, and I don't think anybody can mess that up." Alan poured them both a second glass of wine and directed her to sit at the counter so they could talk while he worked.

"You have a beautiful condo," she said.

"Thank you." He occupied himself heating the oven, turning on burners, and gathering pots, then pulled out ingredients, lining them up on the counter. "I grew up in modest circumstances. I wanted more. I never expected anybody to hand me something for free, and I've worked hard to get where I am today."

"Here you are among the trappings of success, but without anybody to share them with."

"I don't know. I've been so busy, and I haven't thought about it."

"You've never had anything long-term?" She sipped her wine, eyes following what he was doing.

"I've had a few relationships, but nothing I wanted to make permanent."

"Time's a-wasting. You're not getting any younger."

He dumped a jar of spaghetti sauce into a pan.

"Tell me more about your love life," she said.

He chuckled. "You *do* love your sex."

"Love makes the world go round."

"What about you? No one particular person in your life?"

"Without tooting my own horn too much, I like to think of myself as special. I'm looking for a special man, and it would seem that such men are not a dime a dozen. In fact, I would say they're something of a rare breed. Besides," she continued, "I'm following a polyamorous lifestyle at the moment. Monogamy doesn't suit me. But I don't exclude the possibility of finding that special someone and deciding no one else is necessary."

Alan pulled out a loaf of Italian bread and began spreading it with garlic butter. "But your line of work ..."

"Openness and honesty. A truly special partner will understand. A truly special partner will not be possessive or jealous and will put my happiness first."

"You ask for a lot." He placed several pieces of bread on a baking sheet.

"I'm asking for everything. Nothing less will do. A truly special partner will take me on my terms or not at all."

He opened the oven and slid the garlic bread under the grill. "You seem to be at a distance from mainstream society."

"Why not? We only live once. Why not make it a good life?"

He put together two place settings, placing the placemats and utensils in front of her. "I can't argue with that ... How about taking this out and setting it up on the table on the balcony?"

"Well now, doesn't that seem romantic? Dinner overlooking the city!"

Once dinner was ready, they gathered the plates and moved to sit on the balcony. Alan picked up his glass of wine and gestured to her. "Cheers." They clinked glasses.

"Cheers." She looked at her plate. "Aren't *you* the surprise?"

"Like I said, it's nothing special," he said, picking up his cutlery.

"I appreciate the effort. Preparing dinner is an act of kindness and generosity," she said.

"You seem to be a nice person."

"I am."

"You're a little crazy, but nice."

She giggled. "Your idea of crazy is that I don't fit into the usual mold. I'm not your typical everyday woman in our society."

"And what is typical?"

"Wife, mother, subservient, slave, economic dependent with no individual life ..."

"Ouch."

"I'm not condemning men, but our society deserves an overhaul. Unfortunately, inertia is an impediment to social change and society has a tendency to remain as is. Oh, things do change, albeit very, very slowly. Occasionally there's a revolution, but for the most part, the really big changes occur over decades or centuries. It's like the movement of the tectonic plates."

Alan put down his fork and took a sip of wine. "So why don't people do whatever they want to do, social mores be damned?"

"If you do something unacceptable to your peer group, you risk being condemned or ostracized. Heck, you could even be thrown in jail. Consensual homosexual acts between adults are illegal in about seventy countries, for example. The American Psychiatric Association listed homosexuality as a sociopathic personality disturbance until nineteen seventy-four. Some Christian fundamentalists believe homosexuality is a choice or a curable illness. Imagine that — it can be *cured*."

"So, you're pro-homosexual?"

"I see myself as pro-sex. If the people are adults, if the sex is consensual, and if no one is hurt or exploited, the rest of it is none of my business. It's none of the business of society, the state, or the police. Our traditions and our religions have created artificial rules about what's acceptable and what's not.

Consider me simple in my outlook on life: if it feels good, do it."

Alan took his wine glass and leaned back in his chair, watching her with a half-smile.

"You think I'm funny," she said.

"No, I don't."

"Yes, you do. I would have expected it. I'm sure you're more traditional than you even realize." She looked at him wryly. "Are you open and honest?"

"I like to think so."

"You said you masturbate."

"Yes."

"Are you open and honest with your partners?"

"I think so."

"Have you ever masturbated in front of a partner?"

"Uh, no."

"Why not?"

"I guess it's never come up. Partnered sex seems to be about doing things as partners, not as individuals."

"I'm a voyeur and an exhibitionist. If I asked you to masturbate because I wanted to watch, would you do it?"

He tapped his wine glass with one finger. "I don't know."

"If *I* masturbated, would you watch?"

"I suppose."

Hana stifled a laugh. "You men tend to be so visual."

"What's your point in all this?"

"It's simple. Do you feel comfortable enough with yourself and with your partner to do something considered by many — by our society, by our traditions — as bad or at least embarrassing? Do you feel it's normal?"

"I think your point remains elusive."

"Okay. If you take a bath, does it give you pleasure?"

"Yeah."

"Would you take a bath in front of your partner?"

"Uh, I guess."

"If you eat food, is it pleasurable?"

"Yes."

"Would you do it in front of your partner?"

"I think I see where you're going with this." He put down his fork and took a bite of garlic bread.

"So answer me this. Why are these other pleasures okay, but *sexual* pleasure isn't considered normal? It's frowned upon. It's embarrassing. But isn't it natural?"

"Okay," he said. "I can go along with what you're saying ... in theory. But I'm forced to live in a society that doesn't share your outlook on life. Since I'm obliged to live in society, and not obliged to live with *you*, I see myself wanting to conform to society. How did you put it? I run the risk of finding myself condemned or ostracized by my peer group."

Hana nodded. "And there's the rub, so to speak. Our upbringing is affected by our environment, by our society, by our religion, by our community, by our peer group. Without realizing it, without assessing whether it's right or wrong, we've instilled in ourselves a set of guidelines about behavior and morals that govern how we act with others. And I'm not only talking about others in the sense of the public, when we walk around in the streets. I'm talking about our work colleagues, our friends, our family, and our partners — romantic or sexual or both. Yes, when we finally have that intimate relationship with another human being, how we behave is controlled by a lifetime of rules inculcated by our surroundings."

"Oh, come on! Aren't you a tad pessimistic about life?"

She leaned forward, holding her wine glass in one hand and gesturing with the other. "About half of all marriages end in divorce. Why is that? Women initiate two-thirds of all divorces, and you know the number one reason? You might think abuse, but it turns out the number one reason is neglect. They get divorced because their partners are no longer interested in them. Why is that? At one point they got married because they wanted to, they loved one another. But did they *really* get married because they wanted to, or did they do it because it was expected? There's that ideal in our culture of sailing off into a romantic sunset."

Alan smiled.

"What?" she said.

"You're on a roll."

"I'm sorry. I didn't mean to bore you."

"Not at all. You seem to be passionate about this."

"In my work, I've seen stuff. You meet people, you work with people, and after five, ten, twenty times, you see patterns. Instead of seeing one isolated case, you see what I could call statistics and you realize there is a widespread phenomenon here. People are not open and honest. I think they would like to be, but after living a life of lies and deceit, it's hard to change."

He pursed his lips. "Lies and deceit?"

"That makes it sound as though the person in question is bad. I think it comes down to trying to rectify the disparity between how someone thinks they should act and how they want to act."

Taking a sip of wine, Hana leaned back in her chair. "Let me explain. A few years back, I was watching one of those one-on-one talk shows where the moderator had on a guest who was discussing something personal. Now, the show wasn't trashy but it wasn't a big name like *Oprah*. There was a couple discussing being married, family life, and such, but at a certain point, the moderator said that this couple had a secret. After a commercial break, *two women* were sitting there. I looked closer and realized the second woman was the husband in drag. The wife explained that her husband had always had a fetish for women's clothes. Once a month, he dressed up as a female, and the two of them went out to a bar for a drink as if they were girlfriends. She went on to say he was a good husband, a wonderful father to their kids, and a terrific lover, an otherwise exemplary human being, He had this one quirk that was important to his sense of self." She sipped her wine again.

"The human psyche is vast in its variations, and human sexuality is as well. You have to admit that our society frowns upon such behavior. In some groups such behavior would be considered deviant if not punishable by imprisonment."

Alan rubbed his chin and gave her a thoughtful look.

"That's an unusual case."

"Well, we don't *know* that it is, but it does explain the dilemma facing many people. I'm a good person, but I have a quirk. I'm afraid of how others will react if they find out about my quirk, so I keep my mouth shut. I have no idea if there's a statistically significant number of people with the same so-called quirk that would mean it's no longer a quirk, it's normal."

"Dressing up in women's clothes?"

"You never know," she said, smiling. "But I'm talking about sex itself. You have to admit that we shy away from our sexuality. We don't fully embrace it, so there's a lot of ignorance, a lot of misinformation floating around. Many people — *most* people — express some measure of dissatisfaction with their sex lives. I wonder why that is ..."

These ideas were foreign to him, Alan realized, and he didn't know if they were applicable to him. He shrugged. "More wine?"

"Sure."

He stood and took their plates. "I'll be back in a second."

As Alan rinsed off the dishes, he gazed toward the balcony. The sun had set, but the sky was still luminescent and the city lights sparkled in the twilight. It would be a beautiful evening.

"I brought a bottle," he said, stepping back onto the balcony and refilling their glasses. "You've spoken about things I would never have considered."

"When you work with people the way I do, you see the personal side of their lives." She gestured to him. "*You* work with people all the time, as most people do, but *you're* all there for work and that work is your common ground. It's impersonal. It's business.

"With my clients, there's sex, but many more times it's about intimacy with another human being. I'm not talking about romance — it isn't love. I don't love them, and they don't love me. Rather it's about openness, about honesty. We all want to talk about ourselves: our hopes, our dreams, and our desires — even our sexual desires — and we want to do it with someone who is accepting, who isn't judgmental. We want to talk without fear of rejection."

He nodded. "I can see what you're saying."

"Some people can't. Some people *won't*. Some people get so caught up trying to live up to the standards they perceive as being right, they never bother to look to see if those standards are right for *them*."

"You said that."

"Oh? I'm repeating myself. Well, it bears repeating. Some of this goes on without us being aware of it. And even if we *are* aware of it, we may think there's nothing we can do about it, or there may actually be nothing we can do about it."

"What do you mean?"

"Women in our patriarchal society aren't supposed to be sexual. It's that old saying: lady in public, whore in bed. Unfortunately, I think the reality is that women act like ladies all the time and are never whores. It doesn't make for good sex. On the other hand, men aren't supposed to be emotional, soft, cuddly, or sensual — they're supposed to always be the tough guy. That also doesn't make for good sex." She shifted in her chair.

"We learn this behavior from our society, from our environment, and we conform to the norm because we perceive it to be what we should do. We think it's correct or acceptable." Hana took a sip of her wine. "But I could go on and on, and I think I've been doing just that: going on and on and on." She looked out over the city. "It's a nice evening." She stood and leaned against the railing. "God, you have a great view."

He picked up his wine and stood beside her. "I enjoy taking it all in from up here." He pointed to the street. "There are always people walking along the sidewalk. I've got up in the middle of the night to go to the bathroom and peeked out the window to see people going to and fro. Who are those people up at four a.m., and where are they going?"

She nodded, smiling. "The city never sleeps." She put a hand on his shoulder. "You seem like a nice guy."

"Thanks." He half turned and saw that she had started to lean toward him. He moved away. "Don't."

"What?" She raised an eyebrow.

"I feel uncomfortable."

"Ah, well, you're being honest."

"You've been telling me for some time now that we should be open and honest, not hide things."

"Yes, I have."

"So here I am. I feel uncomfortable. Even though I know you're a woman, I'm looking at a man. On top of it, that man is *me*. This is way too weird."

"I don't want you to feel that way. Uncomfortable isn't much fun," she said. "What can I do to assuage those fears? I hope you realize that you're safe. You're protected, among friends. Well ... you're with a friend."

"We just met. We hardly know one another."

Hana took her hand off Alan's shoulder. "Have you ever been on a cruise?"

"Sure, a couple of them."

"Did you meet people, have a good time, go on shore excursions, and share meals with them discussing everything you did that day?"

"Of course."

"They were great people — educated, amusing, intelligent, right? And did you have a warm rapport?"

"Yes."

"And yet you never saw them again."

"Uh, yeah."

Hana smiled. "Why not?"

Alan shrugged. "The cruise was over. We all went back to our lives."

"No exchange of telephone numbers or email addresses? No promises to stay in touch or get together again?"

Alan furrowed his brow. "Well, not really. We shared our time together, then we left and went our separate ways."

"So it's possible to have a moment with somebody, an important moment ..."

"Yes."

"... but a moment that doesn't mean you spend the rest of your lives together."

"Okay. So what's your point?"

"I'm putting forward the idea you can sometimes meet someone, share a moment of closeness and intimacy, possibly but not necessarily including sex, and then never see that person again. That moment is not in any way invalid or any less meaningful than a long-term relationship. This is a saying I love: 'The greatest thing in life is finding people that turn small moments into great moments. Nothing in life must be eternal, only unforgettable.'"

Alan chuckled. "You come across as determined to live life to the fullest."

"And why not? Is there something wrong with that?"

"It's just that ..."

"Just that what?"

"Oh, I don't know. You keep moving me out of my comfort zone."

Hana laughed. "I do like to push people a little." She put her hand back on his shoulder and leaned in so her mouth was close to his ear. She spoke softly. "You're kind of cute, you know?"

Alan didn't move away. He smiled wryly and said, "You're determined to drive me crazy."

"Not at all. I just want you to succumb."

"I thought it was my role as the guy to wear *you* down."

"I would normally say yes, but for some reason, I've wound up taking the lead on this one. All this testosterone must be having an effect on my psyche."

Alan stared at her wide-eyed. "Wait. Are you kidding? I hadn't thought of that. Our minds have been transferred, but are our personalities influenced by the bodies we're in?"

Hana perked up. "That's ... that's an interesting idea. I'm me, but I have to admit that I sometimes recognize I feel different."

"Different how?"

"I'm not sure. I was joking about the testosterone, but maybe, now that I think of it, these bodies *do* have an influence on us, on our behavior and our thinking." She grinned. "Maybe it isn't *me* coming on to you so much as *your body*. Heck, even when your brain isn't around, your maleness continues to be horny. There's that singularity of purpose all men seem to demonstrate."

Alan studied her, half-smiling.

"What?" she said.

"You're enjoying all this."

"Why not? This isn't something that happens to me every day."

"Me neither, thank God." He turned back to the table and gathered up a few things. "Why don't we clean up? If you're up to it, I wouldn't mind going for a walk."

"I'm all yours."

"That's what I'm afraid of."

She snorted.

Alan and Hana strolled through the neighborhood. While the condo building was on a major route filled with shops and restaurants, nearby was residential with tree-lined streets. They started out walking side by side, but at some point, Hana stopped and held out her arm. Alan hesitated at first, then chuckled and took it. They continued walking arm in arm like any normal couple.

"You said you weren't going to do what you do forever," Alan said. "So, what are your plans?"

"I've written a book."

"You have?"

"Yes, there are other things in life I'd like to try. I've worked out a plan to transition to a new career."

"In what?"

"Part of my work is more sexual therapy than escorting. Some men want help with women. Some men want help with sex. Some men want better relationships with their wives and seek my advice on how to achieve that goal. I've even done couples counseling. While escorting is lucrative, I'd like to branch out into other things." She gestured with one hand to emphasize her point.

"The book is about my experiences in sex work, but it's also about my ideas on sex, men and women, and relationships. I'm a feminist, but my approach is all inclusive: we're all in this together. I promote our equality as human beings and I celebrate our differences as men and women."

Alan nodded, half-smiling at her.

"I'm hoping to develop a name for myself as a counselor. I'd like to spread the word and contribute to making the world a better place."

"Is that why you're signed up for a course at Manhattan University?"

She laughed and shook her head. "You really are a snoop. But seriously; I'd like to improve myself, and a few letters after my name would not only make me legal but give me legitimacy. As my editor said—"

"Editor?" he asked.

"I hired a professional editor to work with me and go over the book. I can spellcheck myself, but I need an experienced eye to help me with organization and clarity."

"You seem to be going all out."

"It's worth a shot. This may end up going nowhere, but if I don't try, I'll never succeed."

They went on to speak about many things, to share personal experiences and laugh about the inanities of life. Alan had to admit that he liked Hana. She was different from other people he had met. She was different from other women. Of course, the two of them had been thrown together in the oddest of circumstances, but he wondered what he would have thought if they had met otherwise. What would he have done? What would have happened?

They completed a fair tour of the streets before deciding to call it a night. The next day would be busy, and they had high hopes pinned on the doctor's being able to repeat the crazy miracle that had got them into this mess in the first place. While they had both laughed, their laughter had a nervous ring to it as they wondered what would happen if the doctor failed and they were both forced to remain in each other's bodies for the rest of their lives. Doing it for a day or two had seemed novel. Hana had even said it was a lark. But permanently? That didn't seem funny at all. They would both have to start all over again, and starting over with a new gender seemed unthinkable. The better thing to do was to think positively: the doctor *would* succeed in changing them both back, and they *would* get on with the rest of their lives. They could worry about failure if failure came. In the meantime, they'd focus on success.

Alan announced that he wanted to take a shower before bed, and headed to the master bedroom. He undressed in his walk-in closet and stood looking at himself in the mirror. Staring at the woman's body reflected back at him, he shook his head at the surreal situation. Should he promise to go to church every Sunday if he got out of this mess? He chuckled.

A shower felt good, rinsing away some of the day's tensions. He always liked to wash off the sweat and grime of the day before sliding between clean sheets. Once done, he stopped at the guest bedroom and could hear the ventilating fan from the guest bathroom.

After getting a glass of water, Alan noticed the guest bathroom door was now ajar. He walked by and caught sight of Hana, then stopped and backed up, standing in the darkness as he spied through the gap. She stood naked at the sink, brushing her teeth while shifting around to look at herself from different angles. She leaned forward and spat out the toothpaste before placing the brush back in its holder.

Hana looked down as she ran her hands over herself. She took hold of her penis with her right hand and pulled it aside while using her left hand to cup her scrotum, allowing her a better view. Tilting her head up, she stared at herself in the mirror. She grabbed her penis in a complete grip and moved her hand up and down the shaft. Alan couldn't tear his eyes away. It was mesmerizing to observe her actions and her discovery of his body.

She coughed and the sound woke him from his reverie. He

went back down the hall and finished getting ready for bed. The blinds were drawn, but there was still some light from the street and the occasional muffled sound of a car honking. He rolled onto his side and his thoughts turned to what might happen the next day.

He wasn't sure how long he'd been lying there before he heard the click of his door opening and the bottom of it rubbing along the carpet. He didn't say anything, but sensed a presence. After a moment, the cover was pulled aside and he rolled onto his back. The mattress shifted from the weight of another body.

A minute passed in silence. He perceived movement beneath the covers and a hand brushed against his, wrapping itself around his little finger. It stayed like that for a few seconds, then several fingers slid over his hand. He remained still.

The hand covered his and squeezed. When he didn't respond, the hand squeezed again. He put his thumb on the other hand and squeezed back. The sheet rustled as the body moved against him. He could feel heat radiating onto his skin. The body turned and raised itself. An arm crossed over him and pushed down on the other side. Warm breath touched his lips. There was a subtle male aroma.

Alan shut his eyes. He opened his mouth. He did not push Hana away.

Chapter 11

Alan lay on his side. He didn't know why he had woken at that moment, but a delicious sleepiness permeated his being. He felt good, spent. His sleep was wonderful, and he didn't want it to end yet. Glancing at the clock, he reached behind him and touched the bed. It was empty.

He rolled over and stared at the ceiling. *So, that's what it's like to be a woman.* He let out a big yawn and stretched his limbs before donning a robe and entering the living space.

"Good morning, sleepyhead." Hana sounded cheerful as she moved about the kitchen. He sat down on one of the barstools at the counter and noticed she had set out two place settings and glasses of orange juice.

"You've been busy," he said.

"I woke up this morning and felt absolutely wonderful." She lined up a few eggs beside a frying pan. "Coffee?"

"Sure."

"If I remember correctly, you had the Morning Roast yesterday." Hana set about brewing a cup. "How did you sleep?"

"Like a log."

After the machine made its final whooshing noise, she removed the mug and placed it in front of Alan, leaning over to place her hand on his. Half asleep, he looked up at her. She held his gaze then spoke in a soft, gentle tone. "That was nice." She squeezed his hand and turned her attention back to preparing breakfast.

"How long have you been up?" Alan asked.

"Not long. I had to go to the bathroom and decided to stay up and enjoy the morning."

He sipped his coffee and let a moan of satisfaction escape his lips.

"I made myself a tea and stood out on the balcony," she continued, removing her own cup from the machine. "I'm enjoying that loggia." She held up her cup toward him. "Cheers." She looked around as she took a sip. "Can I get you anything else? Or do you want to wait and wake up?"

"I need to wake up."

"Okay." Hana walked around the counter and stood next to Alan.

He half turned to her. "I ..."

"You want to talk about it?"

"I ... I don't know what to say."

"You're going to analyze it, aren't you."

He looked down, confused about how to proceed.

"Did you have a unique, never-before-in-your-life experience?" she asked.

"Yes."

"Did you enjoy yourself?"

"Yes."

"Did you find it pleasurable?"

"Yes."

"So what's the problem?"

Alan kept looking down.

"Stop it, for crying out loud!" she chided. "It was fun. It was good. I enjoyed you. You enjoyed me. Two people had a good time together. I, for one, would have hated myself for the rest of my life if I had not taken advantage of this once-in-a-lifetime opportunity. Being with a man is one thing, but *being* a man? Oh, wow." She chuckled. "This morning when I peed standing up, it was exhilarating. It felt masculine. Of course, I made a bit of a mess and had to wipe things off afterward." She snickered. "Now I see why some women get ticked off and demand that guys sit. Never mind missing with the first squirt, you splash a lot when hitting the water from two or three feet up. It's hilarious."

Alan managed a half-smile. "A few times I've stood at the toilet before realizing I have nothing to hold onto. Force of habit."

"Ah, we both know the other sex and their idiosyncrasies, but to actually live those idiosyncrasies? Now, *that's* funny."

He shifted on the stool.

"May I do something?"

Alan frowned. "What?"

"I want to kiss you. I'm an affectionate person, and I want to kiss you. We've had a shared experience, and I feel close to you right now."

He looked down at his coffee cup, uncomfortable. "I feel close to you too."

Hana put a hand on the back of Alan's neck. She leaned over and guided his head into position, then pressed her lips against his. She held the kiss before backing away and gazing at him. "I enjoyed that." He remained silent and lowered his eyes. She smiled, let his head go, and stood up. "I'm hungry, so let me get started with those eggs. How about yourself?"

"I'm fine."

"I found frozen bagels." She went to the freezer, dug one out, and defrosted it in the microwave. "You're worried about the gay stuff."

"What?"

"You hesitate because you're worried about anything related to homosexuality."

"Well ..."

"It's okay. I get it. But you have to remember that at the heart of it, I'm a woman and you're a man. Even though we've traded bodies, we still are who we are."

"Yes, I've thought about that."

"We might think of ourselves as more liberated and accepting, but there are undercurrents of our traditions that run deep in our society. Homophobia is one of them. Then again, it all comes back to our prudish outlook on life and all things sexual."

"Uh oh. I hear another one of your lectures coming up."

She chuckled as she fiddled with the toaster. "I can't help myself. This stuff is important to me. It should be important to everyone."

"Have you been with a woman before?"

"Yes, I have."

"Are you Bi?"

She shook her head. "Not really. I'm not particularly

interested in lesbianism, but I do enjoy pleasuring people."

He knitted his brows.

She took a sip of tea. "Years ago, I had a massage from a gay man. He had the most wonderful hands. It wasn't planned, but part-way in he asked if I would like the full treatment and I said yes. He may have been gay — but oh — did that man know his way around the female body! He was amazing. Our time together was about me, all about me, and I couldn't remember the last time I had felt so pampered by a man — or anyone for that matter. I was so deliciously unwound afterward, I think I grinned for two days."

"You have such a sense of freedom. You seem to radiate it. You embrace life and all that it offers."

"Why not? At the heart of it everyone wants the same thing, but we're stymied by our culture."

"Are you always so passionate?"

"Hey, our current culture pisses me off! Racism, sexism, heterosexism, or homophobia; people express fear or hatred of people who are different from them. But what about the big picture? Aren't there far more dangerous issues to be worrying about? The world's filled with pestilence, war, famine, and death, yet people get upset about dumb things." She waved her hand in a sign of resignation.

"Much of our belief system comes from religion. Somebody described Christian fundamentalism as the doctrine that there is an absolutely powerful, infinitely knowledgeable, universe-spanning entity that is deeply and personally concerned with your sex life." She laughed. "We can be such morons."

"We?"

"Hey, I'm not perfect, but I recognize this and try to better myself. There are people, however, who are convinced they're right and everybody else is wrong. These people invariably push their agenda down everybody else's throat. What happened to peace, love, and understanding?"

She went to the stove, turned on a burner, and cracked some eggs into a small dish. "I'm going to make scrambled eggs. Are you sure you don't want any?" She took a whisk and whipped the eggs. "So how do you like being a woman?"

He sipped his coffee and stared off into space, lost in remembering the night. "Well ... uh ... I've always known what it's like to be *in* my partner. Now I understand what it means to have my partner inside of me."

"God, I love a good fuck pounding."

"A good what?"

"I love it when a guy goes into overdrive. I enjoy penetration as much as the next woman, even if it doesn't always get me off. It's exciting to witness somebody losing themselves in a fit of unbridled passion."

"Oh."

She picked up the frying pan and scooped the eggs onto two plates. "Man, did I enjoy my orgasm! I love ejaculating. Heck, I didn't think I was ever going to stop cumming." She let out a guffaw.

"Yes ... uh ... I had a good time, too."

She pointed the spoon at him. "Don't give me that! You had a fabulous time. I have a very responsive body, and you were moaning like there was no tomorrow. You came twice."

Alan felt his face become crimson.

She looked at him and chuckled then walked back around the counter and pulled him off the stool. Wrapping her arms around him, Hana leaned in and kissed him openmouthed. They remained locked in an embrace as she took one arm from his shoulders and ran her hand down the front of his bathrobe. She moved through the folds of the material and reached inside to caress Alan's right breast. "Mmmm," she growled.

Finally, she broke the kiss and held his gaze. She grinned. "I think we're pretty good together." She let him go and sat down. "Let's eat."

After their small breakfast, Alan and Hana went about getting ready, selecting clothes for one another.

"I start with moisturizer," he said examining the various items laid out on the bathroom counter.

She stood behind him, looking at herself in the mirror and

adjusting her collar. "That's right."

He picked up the bottle of moisturizer and unscrewed the top. "This hadn't been on my list of required life skills, but maybe I'm going to be able to say I'm a truly well-rounded man."

"Well-rounded? You missed me having my period last week!"

He stopped and stared straight ahead, dismayed at the thought.

She half smiled. "Are you man enough to be a woman?"

He gave his head a shake then continued his morning ritual.

Hana pulled the looped tie over her head and mimicked Alan's earlier movements by tightening the loop and getting the tie in place. "I'm getting the hang of this." She pulled her collar down and raised her chin to give the knot a final adjustment. "All set."

She watched him go through the steps of getting ready for another day as a woman. "You're doing fine."

Before going out the door, Alan paused in front of a mirror. He smoothed out his skirt and leaned closer to check his makeup. He looked himself in the eye. *What am I doing? Am I getting more womanly?*

Hana held open the door, and the two of them left to meet their fate.

Chapter 12

When Alan and Hana walked into view of Building 42, they saw a large sign taped to the front doors. "Uh oh," Alan said.

He put one hand on the door and leaned closer to read: "The Neuroscience Research Lab is closed until further notice. All work projects are immediately suspended. All employees must turn in their keys and report for reassignment." The note was signed by the chancellor.

Alan tried the door and found it locked. He ripped down the notice and read the text again. "It would seem Blackmore's fears have come true. The chancellor has shut down his research."

"*Now* what do we do?" Hana defiantly held her hands to her hips as she looked around.

He dropped both arms to his sides and released the sign. "Fuck." He closed his eyes and stood motionless. "Blackmore got us into this mess — he's the only one who can get us out of it. We need to find him."

"How?"

"The business card Billy gave us only had the number of the lab. Let's go to the Registrar's office and see if somebody there knows anything about contacting him. Even if the chancellor has it in for Dr. Blackmore, I assume there are some people here who are his friends. We have to find them and get them to help us."

"What about the lab? Isn't the equipment the doctor used locked up in there?"

"Probably. Let's hope that if we find Blackmore, we can also find a way to get him in there to use it."

They went back the way they had come, walking across several open spaces between the university's buildings. At one point, they brushed against each other and Hana took Alan's hand. He gave her a sidelong glance as they stopped to consult a campus map.

"Let's head over there." He pointed off to the right.

She smiled warmly at him and squeezed his hand. "I hope

you don't mind."

"No," he assured her, though he didn't look her in the eye.

The receptionist at the registrar's office couldn't help, but she directed them to an employee administration office down the hall. Alan and Hana found themselves in a small waiting area before a counter, behind which lay an open area with several desks. No one was there. Alan pressed a silver call bell sitting in front of a nameplate that read *Mary Beckett*. He waited at the counter while Hana wandered around looking at various announcements pinned to cork boards.

After a moment, a sober-looking woman came out from a back room. "What do you want?"

Alan smiled. "We're trying to get in contact with Dr. Blackmore."

Mary studied him suspiciously. "We don't hand out personal information."

"I was involved in a test conducted by Dr. Blackmore and would like to speak to him about my results."

"We don't hand out personal information," she said again.

Hana walked up to the counter. "Ms. Beckett?"

Mary turned to her. "Yes, sir. May I help you?"

Hana stuck out her hand. "Alan Maitland. Good to meet you."

Mary looked down at the extended hand and hesitantly shook it.

"Ms. Toussaint and I," Hana said, "were involved in a special test performed by Dr. Blackmore which was not officially sanctioned by the university, and now both of us are facing significant health issues. Dr. Blackmore has to answer for this — he has to be held accountable."

Mary looked startled. "Oh, is *that* the reason the chancellor shut down the research lab?"

"There's only one way to find out, Ms. Beckett. We need to speak directly with Dr. Blackmore and sort this matter out."

"But our policy states—"

"Mary, my health is at stake here." Hana pressed herself against the counter and leaned closer. "I don't only want to do something for myself — I want to do something for others who may have been involved. I don't want to violate the rules and put you in a compromising position. However, may I ask you to call Dr. Blackmore and leave my number? Would you help me out? It's urgent." She held the woman's gaze.

Mary stared back at her, then pulled out a pad and pen. "Jot your number down, but don't tell anybody I did this."

"Mum's the word," Hana said as she pantomimed zipping her lips closed.

Alan wrote down his number. Mary walked over to one of the desks and sat down in front of a computer. After consulting the machine and making several phone calls, she returned to the counter.

"I've called his office, his home, and his cell. Everything is going to voicemail, but I've left your name and number at each place. I'm sure he'll pick up some time."

Hana nodded. "Ms. Beckett, you've been most helpful. I already feel better knowing I'm one step closer to resolving my health issue."

"I hope it's nothing serious."

Hana took hold of Alan's arm and steered him toward the door. "Ms. Beckett, I'm a woman trapped in a man's body."

Alan groaned.

They went down the hall and found a quiet spot. "Who knows if and when he'll get back to us," Alan said, discouraged.

"Should we be concerned?"

"I'd say so, but I'm not sure what else we can do at the moment. We could wander around trying to find him, but since he's not answering his phones, I'm not sure there would be much point. He could be here right now fighting for his academic career before the Board of Regents." He paced and wrung his hands. "This doesn't look good."

She watched him. "Well, instead of sitting here waiting, we could go back to my apartment."

He stopped pacing and sighed. "That's as good an idea as any."

After another train ride across town, they ambled the last couple of blocks to her apartment. This time, he took her by the hand; it seemed like the natural thing to do. It felt comfortable and he wanted to hold her hand in his.

"Why don't you make yourself at home," she said when they entered her apartment. "I'd like to take a moment to check a few things." She got out her laptop and was soon deep in her work.

He walked to the entertainment center and examined the various books. "I'm surprised you can think of anything but our predicament," he said.

"Let's say I'm multitasking. Despite, as you call it, our predicament, I'm still thinking about my ongoing life." She stared at her screen.

He picked up a file folder from a shelf and examined the label. "Who are William and Virginia Howell?" Curious, he opened the folder and glanced at the first page.

"They're a married couple I'm counseling."

"These are your handwritten notes?"

"Yes."

He turned the page. "Mrs. Howell discovered her husband looks at pornography."

Hana didn't look up from her screen as she continued typing. "Yes."

"She thinks her husband's a sex addict?"

"Yes."

"Is he addicted to porn?"

Hana stopped typing and sighed, then got up and walked over to Alan. "That's a bunch of bullshit." She took the folder from his hands and slid it between two tabbed dividers. "There is no such thing as sex or porn addiction. They're nonexistent conditions made up by amateur Puritan psychologists to justify their sex-shaming view of the world."

"But I've seen the term in newspapers."

"It's crap. There are many people living unfulfilled lives and having unfulfilling sex. Show me a man who prefers pornography to a real woman and I'll show you a man who's in a lousy relationship having bad sex." Hana turned to face Alan. "Look at me. Do you think there's even the remote possibility a guy would choose porn over me? Not on my watch!"

"Yes, but you ... well, you have experience ... with other things."

She rolled her eyes. "Good sex isn't just about crazy positions, perverted sex acts, orgies, or whatever you personally interpret from the word 'pornography.' It's about achieving an erotic connection with your partner. The brain is our biggest sex organ: if you go after a person's mind, the body and everything else will follow. Most people have no idea how to do that."

He looked at her with a raised eyebrow.

She stepped close and leaned over his shoulder, brushing her lips along his cheek before speaking softly in his ear. "I can give you an erection without touching you." He felt her warm breath on his skin. "I can even make you cum without touching you." Hana paused then puckered her lips next to his ear, quietly making the smacking noise of a kiss. Alan shivered.

She stood up and looked him in the eye. "You've never talked?"

"Pardon?"

"You've never had phone sex?"

"No."

"You've never sexted?"

"No."

"You've never had an erotically charged exchange of emails or letters with another person?"

"Uh, no."

"Sex isn't just an act," Hana said. "It isn't just about technique, caresses, and positions. Sex is very much about communication. Foreplay can be an email or text or a phone call or recorded message. Sex is all about imagination, and exchanging those ideas with your partner. Have you ever told your fantasies to anybody?"

"Hmmm ... I guess not."

"Why not? Why not share yourself? Why not share the

more personal part of you?"

"I'd feel uncomfortable."

"We're back to our fear of criticism, of judgment. We can't be open and honest with our partner. Heck, we can't even be open and honest with *ourselves*. Mr. and Mrs. Howell are completely lacking in communication both in the bedroom and outside it, another typical modern-day couple. William doesn't want to look at porn — he wants to have good sex with his wife. Since he's not getting good sex, he's looking for an outlet elsewhere. Virginia grew up in a Puritan-like family: only missionary sex and only for procreation. She'd better wake up, or she could lose her husband. He's not a pervert or a sex addict or whatever — he's just a man who wants to have a deep and lasting erotic connection with his partner. Period."

She returned to her computer and gazed once again at the screen.

Alan furrowed his brow. "I ... I never thought about that."

"Stop thinking about fucking my body and start thinking about fucking my mind." She focused on her work.

A buzzer sounded on the other side of the room. Alan looked toward it.

"Would you answer that?" Hana asked.

He walked over to the wall panel and pressed the *View* button. The display panel showed a woman standing at the front door. "Are you expecting anybody?"

"Not that I remember."

He pressed *Talk.* "Hello?"

The woman leaned in and said, "It's me, Hana. Let me up."

"Who?"

"It's Kim, ya big silly. Let me in."

Alan turned around. "Who's Kim?"

Hana didn't look up. "She's a friend. Let her in."

He spoke into the device—"Come on up" — and pressed *Unlock.* "Is there anything I should know?"

She shrugged and kept typing. "Kim's an escort. We've done business together."

Alan stood at the door, wondering what that meant. He

heard footsteps in the hall and a knock at the door. After unlocking the deadbolt and pulling the door open, he faced a blonde woman, who grinned back at him. Kim pulled open her long coat to reveal her naked body, except for stockings and a garter belt.

"Ta-da!" she said with an enthusiastic cry.

He stood there, frozen, looking the woman up and down.

"Well, what do you think?"

He continued to stare.

"Mr. Bobby wanted to take me to dinner tonight, so I thought I'd bring out my best. The idea of me being like this under my coat drives him wild!" Kim continued to hold the coat open, a look of triumph on her face.

"Yes," Alan said. "That is, uh, quite the outfit."

She wrapped herself back up and stepped into the apartment. "The old saying is true: less is more. And to that I would add that while what you can't see won't hurt you, what you *can't* see will spark the imagination."

Alan shut the door just as Kim noticed Hana.

"Ooh, what's this?" She strode over to the table and stood beside Hana, pulling open her coat and cocking one leg. "Well, what do you think?"

Hana stopped typing and looked up at her. She chuckled. "Yes, I can see that will drive Mr. Bobby wild."

Kim shot Alan a glance. "See? Here's the unbiased opinion of a man." She closed her coat and did up a button.

Hana stood and took Kim's hand, kissing it and keeping her eyes on the other woman. "A pleasure to meet you."

Kim grinned. "Well, aren't *you* the charmer."

Hana slid an arm around Kim's waist and pulled her close. She put her face up to Kim's and spoke softly: "A man has to do what a man has to do."

Kim stared at Hana, their faces almost touching. They remained silent until Kim put one hand between Hana's legs and felt her up. "No gun. So you really *are* happy to see me."

Hana laughed and let her go.

Kim glanced back at Alan. "You never bring clients here, so

this must be personal." She grasped Hana's left biceps. "I'm impressed."

"Let's say it's mutual," Hana said.

Kim kept her eyes on her. "I do believe your man is flirting with me. Mister ...?"

"Alan Maitland."

Kim ran a hand down the lapel of Hana's suit. "Nice manners. Nice suit. Are you the whole package, Mr. Maitland?"

"This poor boy does what he can."

Kim looked at Hana curiously. "You're here. In this apartment. That unto itself is significant. But 'poor boy'? I'm certain you're underselling yourself, but your presence makes me think you overdeliver. I like humility, but I do *so* like strength."

Kim turned and walked back to Alan, brandishing a piece of paper. "I have here, Hana, your ticket for the Saturday-night fête of all fêtes. Why don't I walk over and the two of us can take a cab? No sense in each of us going separately."

Alan took the ticket. "Uh, yeah, sure." He waved it at Hana with a questioning look.

"So the two of you are off to the McConnell shindig," Hana said.

Kim spun around. "Why, yes. Do you know it?"

"I'm familiar with it."

"Oh really? Now, would we be having the pleasure of your company?"

"Alas, this year my name did not find its way onto the guest list. I'm afraid my Saturday night will be more mundane."

"Oh, pooh." Kim pouted. "But there *is* the rest of the year, and there'll be other parties." Walking to the door, she said to Alan, "Let me know if you ever decide to treat him to a threesome. I'd like to see him with his clothes off." She pulled the door open. "Ta ta, you two. Don't do anything I wouldn't do!" she called out, before disappearing down the hallway.

Alan held the ticket up to Hana.

"Anthony McConnell," Hana said, "is the very, very wealthy head of the Perry Investment Group."

"I know the name. You travel in impressive circles."

"He's a fun guy who enjoys his wealth and everything it can buy. I've had the pleasure, as has Kim. Every year he throws a party for all his wealthy friends, renting out an entire floor of the St. Regis. I think, in a way, Anthony likes to let everybody know who's top dog. He likes to invite along some of his former dates to pepper the party with unattached females."

Alan set the ticket on the table. "You go there to do business?"

"No, I go to have a good time, but it's a good way to make contacts. Not all clients are rich, but if I had a choice, they would be. It's interesting how the wealthy look at life — when you're not counting pennies, your approach to life and pleasure can be quite different. There are people out there who throw around a thousand dollars the way you or I would consider a dime."

"So, who's Kim?"

Hana chuckled. "Kimberly Adler, a fun personality. I mentored her and helped her move into the upscale market. Like me, she thoroughly enjoys working with people. She likes to have a good time, and she likes making sure other people have a good time too. As you can see, she's very much the flirt."

"*She's* the flirt? What the heck were you doing?"

"What?" Hana feigned innocence then smiled. "I'm getting a kick out of being a guy, and what better way than to try it out with somebody I know?"

"Yeah, yeah. But I have to admit I felt a twinge of jealousy."

Hana laughed. "It's all in good fun. Kim likes to test boundaries, but she's a respectful person. She would never do anything to make anybody uncomfortable."

"A threesome?"

She shrugged. "We've had some interesting adventures together."

"I'm not sure I want to ask."

"If you would consider letting go of the moral shackles of

traditional society, you may find there is a magical world of not just mutual pleasure, but respect, friendship, and love." Hana slipped one arm around Alan's waist and said, "I'm still your guy. Or girl. Or maybe both at the same time."

"It's not very dull with you around."

She leaned over and kissed the top of his head.

"Am I going to get used to that?" he asked.

She chuckled. "I'll wear you down."

A muffled buzz interrupted them. "My phone!" Alan sprang for his purse and dug around for the device. "Hello? Hello?" He studied the display. "Shit. I missed it. It's gone to voicemail." He punched a few keys and held the device to his ear as he paced. *Call me. It's urgent.*

"It's Dr. Blackmore," he said.

"Good."

"He says it's urgent."

"As in, he can't change us back?"

"I'm going to phone him." He punched some buttons and listened. "I'm going to put it on speaker. Come over here." He held the device in front of him as she stood close.

There was a click on the line, and a somewhat indistinct voice said, "Hello?"

"Dr. Blackmore?" Alan said. "It's Alan and Hana."

"I'm in trouble. The lab's been shut down."

"We know."

"Oh. You were there, as we planned."

"Yes. And we read the closure notice taped to the door." Alan looked at Hana. "What's going on?"

"I'm adjunct faculty, and I don't have a contract with the university. I serve at the pleasure of the chancellor. Right now, he's none too pleased with me, and he's decided the money allocated for my research can be better spent elsewhere."

"Wait," Alan said. "He can't stop your work in the middle of this test! What about us?"

"Everything we need is in that laboratory, but ..."

Alan and Hana looked at each other. "But what, Doctor?" Hana said.

"The chancellor has closed the doors, but that's not all. At nine o'clock tomorrow morning, a crew will be in to dismantle the entire operation and remove all equipment. In less than twenty-four hours, there will no longer be any means of reversing the effects of your condition. You'll be obliged to live out the rest of your lives as you are right now."

There was dead silence in the room. After a few seconds, the doctor said, "Are you still there?"

"Jesus," Alan said. "I think we're both shocked into silence. Having to remain as we are permanently is inconceivable."

Hana leaned over and whispered in his ear, "No shit."

He waved his hand at her then put his finger to his lips.

"I have a theory," Blackmore said. "A chip can be set to do a data dump. Normally, this transfers data from the chip to the scanner so the computer can analyze it. I suspect that the data dump function got turned on and the chip overwrote your minds. The wifi connection to our central computer provided incremental updates to both your chips, keeping them in sync with the other's brain until the switch occurred. I can duplicate this configuration, and we can see what happens. That's my theory. It's untested, but I would say that there's no other option. It's this or stay as you are."

Alan glanced at Hana. "We're both of the mind to do whatever it takes to correct this. We don't care about the risks. We don't have any other choice," he said. "What are you proposing?"

"I'll meet you tonight at ten, behind the building. I have keys for the basement door closest to the lab. It's unlit and dark. We can evade security patrols and get into the building for our last opportunity to use the equipment before it's gone."

"Okay, Dr. Blackmore. We'll be there. Is there anything else we can do to assist?"

"At this stage of the game, all you can do is cross your fingers."

Chapter 13

Alan and Hana were on edge. It was done — decided. They had set a specific time to meet the doctor and, they hoped, to implement the solution to their dilemma. There was nothing else to do but try to keep themselves busy for a few hours.

Alan's phone rang and he frowned at the display. "Oh boy, it's Jack. What does he want?"

"Why don't you answer it?"

"I'll let it go to voicemail then listen to the message. The less you talk to him the better."

"What? I thought I did a terrific acting job."

"You're going to get me in trouble." He waited for the voicemail notification then called up the message. He held the device to his ear and listened. "Oh my God." He gasped and looked at the time.

"What?"

"I have to go to the office."

"Now?"

"Yes, right now."

"First you complain about my acting job, and now you want to put me right in the middle of the lions' den?"

"I don't have a choice. I'll grab my purse and we're out of here."

When he heard Hana chuckle, he realized what he'd just said, and he couldn't help but chuckle too.

"What's the big deal?" she asked as they hurried out onto the street and headed to the subway.

"I have important responsibilities at the company, and those responsibilities sometimes involve face time."

"I thought these days, with the Internet and all that, almost everyone could work remotely from anywhere."

"You get that impression, but the world still works for the most part by shaking a real person's hand. This afternoon, there's a foreign group of investors visiting the company. The president's making a pitch for their business, and I'm involved in preparing a custom investment plan tailored to their particular needs in our national market. They're hoping to expand their operations to North America, and my company would like the job of giving them a foothold here in the United States."

"Sounds impressive. But I thought you were sick."

"For the staff — for Jack and the boys and pub night — yes, I'm sick. But for something like this, I can't be. This is the big time, and deals stop for no man. Or woman." Alan cast a glance at Hana. "But if I can be serious for a moment: this is a very important deal. This is my work. This is my career. I don't know if I can fully impart to you the value of this afternoon's handshake. I want you to treat this with the utmost seriousness. You can fool around with Jack, but you can't fool around *here*."

"I'll do my best," Hana said. "Let's hope my best is good enough."

"Here's my plan. You'll stay in my office as much as possible and not wander around. That way we can minimize your contact with other staff. I don't want people to think I'm acting oddly. I'll be an outside research partner and stay by your side as an assistant in putting together the proposal. My presence won't be questioned and will look normal. This way, I can guide you, give you the names of people, describe what's going on, and suggest things to say."

"Ooh, this sounds like fun!"

"Fun?" He gave her a glance and found she was grinning. He shook his head. "You're going to shave years off my life."

They arrived in the heart of the financial district and exited into an underground concourse. People were everywhere. Alan led them through a maze of passageways populated by shops and fast food outlets to the main elevators of the tower where his company had offices.

When the elevator doors opened at the lobby level, a crowd of people streamed in and everyone shifted to make room. Alan found himself pushed up against a bald, middle-aged man and immediately had the feeling that the man was ogling his breasts. When Alan glanced up at the man, he looked away.

Okay, baldy — what's the deal? At the next bell chime, Alan again glanced up at him, but this time it took a second for the man to notice Alan was looking. Before the man looked away, Alan realized that he *was* staring down his blouse, and discreetly checked to see if he had one too many buttons undone. Was he exposing too much cleavage? He'd wanted to dress in a business-like manner, but had he overlooked something? Alan attempted to turn away, but the car was so packed, he could hardly move.

The crowd thinned out at each stop, and the man finally got off at the nineteenth floor. Alan was glad to see him go. *Let baldy get his jollies elsewhere,* he thought.

After Alan and Hana got off at the twenty-eighth floor, he turned to her and whispered, "That guy was ogling me."

"Who?"

"The guy in the elevator."

"So?"

"I felt uncomfortable." He swiped his security card and they entered the company offices.

"It happens. You were jammed together face to face."

"Yeah, but I thought he was staring down my blouse."

She shrugged. "Why not? You've got nice tits."

"Do I have too many buttons open?"

"No, you look fine."

"Still ..."

"Still what? Guys like women. Guys look at women. Guys chase women."

"I guess," Alan said. "I hadn't thought about it before in terms like that. When you're the target, the practice becomes so much more obvious."

"You lead a sheltered life. I'll take you out to a Chippendales show so you can witness first-hand a bunch of women in heat. Talk about role reversal! Heck, with your bod, I could put *you* up on stage. You develop a different perspective on sexual attraction when you have a roomful of strangers lusting after your body. We don't want your brains — we want your brawn."

He looked at her askance as he steered her into his office, then sat down and switched on the computer. Hana walked around the office, examining framed diplomas and looking at the scribbling on a whiteboard.

"So this is where it all happens," she said.

He concentrated on the screen and made no comment.

She walked over to the window and took in the view. "Wow. You really are up here."

"I like it."

She stood with her back to the room as he remained focused on his computer.

"We have a new employee?" someone said.

He looked up to find Fred sticking his head through the doorway. Hana turned around and smiled. "Hey."

"I hope she's not stealing all our company secrets," Fred said.

"Not at all," Hana said. "She's been helping me with the proposal, and I thought I'd invite her along for this afternoon's meeting."

"Really?"

Alan got up, holding a piece of paper, and walked over to Hana. "Did you see this?" He stood with his back to the door, holding the paper before her and whispered, "Fred."

"No, I didn't," she said. Without pausing, she smiled at the man in the doorway. "Oh, Fred, I'd like you to meet Hana Toussaint."

Fred stepped into the room and stuck out his hand. "Pleasure."

Alan shook the proffered hand and smiled. "Hello, Fred."

"Too bad you missed the pub night, Alan." Fred watched Alan walk back around the desk and resume his work, then smiled at Hana and gave an approving nod. "Too bad you were, uh, *sick*." He looked between Alan and Hana. "I can see how you've been tied up."

Hana grinned. "A guy's gotta do what a guy's gotta do."

"Good luck this afternoon," Fred said as he started for the door.

"Thanks," Hana said.

Fred stopped in the doorway and looked again at Alan. He grinned at Hana and gave a thumbs up sign, then disappeared down the hall.

"I think your coworkers approve of your new girlfriend."

"What?" Alan, distracted, consulted the screen and scanned the various papers laid out on the desk. "Thank God I completed this days ago. Considering my preoccupation with our current problem, I never would have gotten this done." He typed furiously. "We have thirty minutes before the presentation."

"I'm ready when you are," Hana said. "Come to think of it, I'm as ready as you are."

He remained fixated on the computer. "I sent the final copy to print. I have to visit the restroom, so I'll pick it up on the way back. Do you want anything?"

"Like what?"

"A tea? I thought I'd stop and get a coffee in the kitchen."

"Yes, I'd love a tea."

"I'll shut the door to reduce the possibility of somebody stopping by to talk with you."

"I feel like such a leper," she said.

Alan gave her a wry smile, picked up a coffee mug from the desk, and headed down the hall. He put his hand on the men's room door before correcting himself and going to the women's. Setting the mug down on the counter, he went to the nearest stall and studied the toilet seat. How many times had he been grossed out by a seat peppered with piss? Able to stand up, most men couldn't be bothered to lift the seat — and with the world's worst aim, they made a goddamn mess. Most wouldn't clean up after themselves, either. Were women any better? At least here, in the company washroom, things seemed to be clean.

He lifted his skirt, pulled down his pantyhose and panties, and sat down. *My kingdom for a urinal,* he thought as he pulled off some toilet paper. Alan couldn't help but reflect on the logistics of a woman using a urinal. He could think of many questions: Was it even possible? Should he find an empty men's room and try? Should he ask Hana?

The door to the washroom opened and somebody entered. Alan heard running water. Finishing his business, he flushed and stood up. He stepped out to wash his hands and recognized Adrienne, an administrative assistant, freshening up.

He leaned over to turn on the water and washed his hands.

"Isn't that Alan Maitland's coffee mug?"

He glanced in the mirror at Adrienne. "Yes."

"I thought I knew it."

Alan finished and turned off the water, pulling a paper towel from the wall dispenser.

"I don't think I've seen you around here before," Adrienne said.

"Just here for the day."

Adrienne nodded and finished applying lipstick before leaving.

Alan stood there, looking at himself in the mirror. A thirty-something professional-looking woman stared back at him. He shook his head then picked up the mug and stopped. The memory of Adrienne checking her make-up stuck in his head. He leaned over the sink and looked at his face, studying his own. *Good? Bad? In need of freshening up?* He thought about the number of things he had to take into account being a woman. It all seemed so complex. *What if I have to do this for the rest of my life?* He shuddered, picked up the mug, and left.

The lunchroom was empty. He filled the mug with tea and found a spare for his coffee. He headed back to his office by way of the printer and tucked his report under one arm then picked the mugs back up.

He paused outside the closed door of his office. He could hear laughter inside. This couldn't be good. He tapped the door with his foot and the talking stopped. There was a moment of silence before the door swung open. Hana stood there with a big smile. "Ms. Toussaint, come in. I'd like to introduce you to Henry Fagler."

He gaped. Henry Fagler was the president of the company. He knew of the man but had never met him before, and now, Hana was chatting with him as if they were old buddies.

"Do come in," she said.

Alan stepped into the office and handed her the tea. He reached out to shake hands. "Mr. Fagler."

"Ms. Toussaint. Alan was telling me you will be joining him this afternoon in assisting me with the presentation."

"Yes, sir."

"I appreciate all the help we can get. This is an important contract, and I'm hoping we convince the European delegation we are the firm they should choose."

"I — we will do our best, sir." Alan glanced at Hana. What had she been saying to this man? How did she develop such a close rapport with a total stranger? He tried to control his surprise and remain calm.

"Alan, it's been great talking with you," Fagler said. "I look forward to your presentation in—" He glanced at his watch. "In ten minutes, to be exact."

Hana smiled. "Thank you. We're going to win this." She shook hands with Fagler and walked him to the door.

After the man had gone, Alan stared at her, wide-eyed. "What in heaven's name did you do? I go out for a few minutes and you're buddy-buddy with the president of the corporation?"

She shrugged. "He popped in to say hello before the meeting. It was the usual small talk about the weather and such. When he mentioned feeling a little sore after going to the gym, I told him a joke."

"Which was?"

"I said to the gym instructor, 'Can you teach me to do the splits?' He said, 'How flexible are you?' I said, 'I can't make Tuesdays.'" She grinned. "That got him howling and the rest, as they say, is history. Pull off this presentation and land this contract, and I think you'll get yourself a raise. Maybe a promotion. Oh hell, let's go for both!"

"I think you're getting ahead of yourself."

"I like to be positive. The little engine that could and all that."

Alan checked the time. "Okay. Let's go."

They arrived a few minutes early and found an assistant doing a last check of the projection system. Fagler arrived a minute later with the European group, chatting with one man in particular.

"Alan, please come over and let me introduce you," Fagler said, gesturing to Hana.

Alan didn't dare move, as he had to defer to Hana — to himself. He was a subordinate now, after all.

Fagler smiled as he turned to her. "Alan, I'd like you to meet Marcel Dassault. Marcel, this is Alan Maitland, the investment analyst who put together our proposal."

"Monsieur Dassault, bonjour." Hana smiled as she shook his hands.

Dassault nodded. *"Monsieur Maitland."*

Hana gestured toward a side table and posed a question in French.

"Merci," Dassault said.

Hana led the man over to the table and assisted him in getting a cup of coffee. Alan noticed that Fagler watched her with a sly smile.

It took a few minutes to get people set up with refreshments before Fagler said, "If everyone would like to take a seat, we can get started with our presentation." An assistant dimmed the lights, and the first slide of the presentation projected onto a drop-down screen at one end of the room. Over the next ten minutes, Fagler made the case for the company's proposal, then opened the floor to questions. Dassault spoke up first to thank Fagler for his presentation, and talked about his company and its future in North America. He then turned to address Hana.

"Mr. Maitland, what are your thoughts on the bank rates over the next five years?"

Alan felt his insides tighten. How would they get out of this sticky situation?

"It's a difficult question to answer with one hundred percent certainty," Hana said. "If I may, Ms. Toussaint has prepared a presentation about the complexities of rates."

Alan was both surprised and delighted. Hana had cleverly passed the question over to him, without giving the slightest indication that she was incapable of answering. He rose and confidently gave his thoughts on the subject, concluding by pointing out that his remarks could also be found in the appendix to the proposal.

With the proceedings finished, everyone at the table stood and shook hands. Dassault said he would phone his head office to discuss the proposal and would give Fagler his answer forthwith.

On the way out, Dassault shook Hana's hand a second time. *"Monsieur Maitland, merci beaucoup."*

"Je vous en prie." She smiled and nodded to the man.

Fagler showed the visiting group to the elevator while Hana and Alan headed back to his office.

"You carried yourself very well," Alan said.

"I bet you say that to *all* the girls who take over your body."

He chuckled. "Seriously — you did a good job back there. And I appreciate your deftness in bringing me into the conversation."

"Both of us did a good job. You wrote the proposal."

Fagler stuck his head in the door. "Alan, I had no idea you spoke French!"

"Enough to get myself into trouble."

"It's the type of thing that can make or break a negotiation. All the companies in contention have proposals as good as ours, so it can be something as insignificant as talking to somebody in their native language that may warm them up. Great job. Thanks." Fagler slapped the doorframe to emphasize his last word and disappeared.

Hana pointed at Alan. "You thought I was being funny before. I think you may get something out of this."

"I'm not counting my chickens before they're hatched, but yes, I have a good feeling. Of course, you've now put the pressure on me to learn French."

"I can help you out."

Alan straightened out a few papers and turned off his computer. "I don't know about you, but I could use a bite to eat. How about we find ourselves a terrace somewhere and enjoy life?"

Hana giggled. "I think you finally understand my approach to life: eat dessert first."

They headed down the hall to the elevators, but before Alan hit the down button, Jack came around a corner.

"Hey, Alan, Hana. I heard you did a good job with the proposal this afternoon."

"News travels fast," Hana said.

"Yes, it does. You speak French? You've never mentioned that before."

"It's never come up."

"I was surprised when I heard that. I've known you for a few years now, and I'd have thought I'd have known."

"Do you speak French?" Hana asked.

Jack shifted his gaze. "Uh, no."

She chuckled. "There's your answer. Why would I ever speak French to you if you don't speak French?"

"Oh, yeah. Right."

"Besides, I'm not very good. I know enough to get by, but that's about it. Trust me — spouting off a few words is nothing to brag about."

Jack nodded. "So where are the two of you off to?"

"Somewhere out there," Hana said, "is a terrace with our name on it."

"Happy hunting."

Hana pushed the elevator button. "See you."

As the elevator doors slid closed, Alan turned to Hana. "You were good back there."

"Thanks."

"You're good with people."

Hana glanced at him. "I enjoy people. I enjoy working with them. Boardroom, bedroom — it's all about breaking the ice, stroking the ego, and building trust. And I'm not just talking about men. Those ideas are applicable to both men and women. It's human nature — we all want to feel important."

Alan smiled and nodded in agreement.

"I have a few tricks up my sleeve," she said.

"So I see."

Chapter 14

At this hour, the university quadrangle was an oasis of calm surrounded by a still-bustling city. Besides a few evening lectures, classes were over. Other than the pub and the student council offices, nothing appeared to be open. Alan and Hana strolled hand in hand across the grounds looking like any other couple. From time to time, they saw a security guard on patrol, but there didn't seem to be too many of them. They hoped this wouldn't prevent them from gaining access to the lab as Dr. Blackmore had promised.

When they arrived at Building 42, there was nobody around. They made their way down a slope to the back of the building. Alan led the way, and when they rounded the last corner, he stopped abruptly, causing Hana to run into him. He pushed her back around the corner.

"What's the matter?" she whispered.

"There are two security guards back there having a smoke."

She snuck a look. "I wonder where Blackmore is."

"I don't know, but we aren't going to get in there any time soon if those two yahoos keep goofing off."

Hana chuckled. "Yahoos?"

"What? Shouldn't they be doing their rounds?"

"As opposed to ... bothering us?"

"That's right." Alan peeked around the corner. "Damn. Now what are we going to do?"

There was a noise nearby: *psst.*

"Did you hear that?" she said.

"Hear what?"

Once again, there was the same noise: *psst.*

"That noise."

The two of them turned to stare at a clump of bushes.

"I think it came from there," Hana said, pointing to the dark shrubs. She took a few tentative steps in that direction until a soft voice said, "Come here." Hana motioned for Alan to follow. They moved away from the building, making sure to stay hidden from the guards.

A voice from the darkness said, "It's Blackmore."

"I gather you saw the guards," Alan said.

"Yes. I'm trying to be extra careful. If the chancellor has closed the lab, I'm guessing he's had me declared persona non grata on campus, and I don't want to risk being escorted off the grounds by security. I can't stroll out in the open like you two can. I have to move in the shadows."

"Sounds kind of cloak and dagger," Hana said.

"I suppose, and in any other circumstances I might find it amusing. Just not now." Blackmore shook his head and clicked his tongue. "Before we can get into the building, we need to get rid of those two guards."

"Why don't we go in the front entrance?" Alan asked.

"The lab is at the back. When I turn on the equipment, I'm afraid those guards will see the lights and investigate."

"Leave it to me," Hana said, motioning to Alan. "I should say, leave it to *you*."

He scowled. "What are you babbling about?"

"You have feminine wiles. Use them."

"What?"

She took his hand and led him a few paces away so the light from a streetlamp shone on them. She undid the top two buttons of the blouse he wore and pulled the material aside.

He looked down. "Oh, you've *got* to be kidding me."

"Not the least bit." She inspected his cleavage and undid a third button, ensuring that the V of the neckline plunged low enough to show an expanse of breasts and the edge of the lacy bra. "There," she said. "I guarantee they'll never look you in the eye." She chuckled.

"You're not suggesting I go down there and distract them, are you?"

"Not distract them, but lead them away."

"Lead them where?"

"Anywhere. Then hightail it back here as quickly as possible." Hana glanced downward. "And one other thing. Walk with more hip motion. Give us some of your sexiness."

"This is setting feminism back decades," Alan said.

"When you're swimming in a pool full of sharks, you behave accordingly. Right now, we need a little blood in the water to get their attention."

"It can't be this easy."

"Nobody's forcing those men to take the bait. Heck, if they're both gay, this won't work at all." She stepped back and looked him up and down. "You want to hook the fish and reel them in. You've got breasts, hips, a pretty face, and a feminine voice. Use them all and make sure you lead them *away* from this building."

Alan again looked down at the plunging V of his blouse. "I can't believe I'm doing this."

"Get going. We're counting on you." Hana gave him a gentle push toward the guards.

Alan walked around the corner and clicked his tongue at the absurdity of his predicament. His mind buzzed as he tried to work out a strategy for getting the attention of the two guards and leading them away from the rear entrance. He thought of the femmes fatales he had seen in movies and on TV. He had even watched this scene play out in bars. Now he was going to do the same? He ran his left hand down the lapel of his blouse and felt the exposed curve of his breast. Were men really that easily led astray by the female form?

The two guards stood close to a street lamp, chatting. One would raise a hand to take a drag and pass the cigarette to the other. The smell of marijuana wafted along the path. Both guards peered into the darkness at the sound of footsteps, the click of heels on concrete. Alan sashayed into sight.

"Gentlemen, I seems to have missed t'party," he slurred, having decided at the last minute to pretend he was tipsy. He stood in front of the guards. The street lamp shone down like a spotlight, and the guards had a clear view. He glanced at the first guard then at the second. He noticed that neither one of them was looking him in the eye. *Never underestimate the power of cleavage.*

He pointed back toward the campus. "I thinks I missed da pub somewhere back there." He shifted his weight and his ankle twisted, causing him to take a step to regain his balance. *Goddamn high heels.* One of the guards grabbed his arm to help steady him.

"Careful," the guard said. "Don't trip on the sidewalk."

"Thanks you. Perhaps you kind enoughs show where I'm supposed go?" The guard was staring at his chest. *Up here, buddy.*

"Sure. I was just finishing up here and need to get back to my rounds." The guard pointed along the walkway. "Let's head back up this way."

"Thank you, kind sir." He noticed that the guard still had a hold on his arm.

Alan and the guard took a few steps before Alan realized the second guard wasn't following. He stopped and gestured to him. "Wait. Don't I get *two* escorts, one for each arm?" The guard was still puffing on the joint. "Come here," Alan said, and offered his other arm. The man smiled, took a long last toke, and threw the remainder of the roach away. Alan slid an arm through his.

"This lady is well protected tonight," he said, and giggled. "Let's find that party!" The three headed up the path.

Alan chatted with the two guards and learned more about Alvin and Ted than he cared to know. They led him to the campus pub, and he slurred his appreciation as he stepped inside, the guards walking off in the opposite direction. He buttoned up his blouse as he peeked outside. When the guards disappeared around a corner, he retraced his steps to the lab.

Once there, he knocked on the door and waited. A moment later he knocked again, but this time tapping out the rhythm: *Shave and a haircut, two bits.* The door opened.

"Thank God, it's you," Hana said. "I was worried it might have been another security guard."

Alan stepped inside and she pulled the door shut tight.

"How did it go?" Hana asked.

"Mission accomplished," Alan said. "I never appreciated how predictable men are. We really do go for tits."

"One of my favorite ploys," Hana said, chuckling. "But

don't forget, we gals have our hot buttons too. Just different ones." She led him down the hall. "Where did you go?"

"I had them lead me back to the campus bar," Alan said.

They entered the lab and saw the beam of a flashlight moving around in one corner. There was a thud and Blackmore cursed in the darkness. "I can't see a damn thing."

"Can we help?" Alan asked.

"You wouldn't know what to do." He shone his flashlight at them. "No offense."

"None taken."

Blackmore made his way back to them. "The first step is to remove the existing chips."

"Is this going to hurt?" Hana said, sounding worried.

He shrugged. "It's like a pinprick."

"What about bleeding?"

"Sometimes, yes. As with any needle injection a bandage may be necessary to stop some initial bleeding, but most of the time a minute or two of applied pressure is sufficient." The doctor pulled up a metal chair. "Alan — I mean, Hana, I want you to sit." He handed Alan the flashlight. "Hold this."

Hana sat down. Blackmore fiddled with the controls of a small device and said, "Tilt your head forward." He examined the exposed back of her neck. Alan shone the flashlight on the area and thought he could see discoloration on the skin. Blackmore held the device over her neck and watched a small display. It showed crosshairs and targeted a spot that Alan figured was the implant. The doctor moved the device until the spot was in the middle of the display and pressed a button. There was a slight noise, and she said, "Ow."

Blackmore said to her, "Give me your hand." He guided it into place over the mark on the back of her neck. "Now apply some pressure."

Blackmore moved to a side table and held the device over a small glass dish. "Bring the light over here," he said to Alan. He pressed another button, and something tiny fell into the dish. Alan leaned over to look at it.

"That's the chip?"

"Yes. It's no bigger than a grain of rice." Blackmore again fiddled with the device. "Now, Alan, let's do the same for you."

Blackmore got Hana to stand and hold the flashlight with her free hand as he got Alan into position. They went through the same procedure and soon both Hana and Alan stood with their hands on the backs of their necks.

"I need to examine each of the chips. I don't want to take any chances, so I'm going to double-check everything." Blackmore took the flashlight from Hana and headed to the computer station. "Would one of you hold this flashlight for me?" They walked over to watch the doctor work and Alan held the light over the table.

"I want to use the chip reader to look at the contents of the micro-system. As I said, the chips were seeded with a snapshot of your brains. As the chips operate, they incrementally update that information with new data. In theory, what's on the chip, coupled with the updates, is a snapshot of your brain as it is right now. Well, up to the point when I removed them from you."

Blackmore pulled out a small black box with a cable connecting it to the computer. "Oh, wait. I need those two dishes with your chips." The doctor stood and took the flashlight from Alan. He made his way back to the other table and picked up the two dishes. There was a thump followed by two sharp rings.

Alan and Hana watched as the flashlight pointed down. "Oh crap," Blackmore said. "I banged into a table and dropped the dishes." The light moved closer to the floor as the doctor crouched over the area. "Thank God they didn't break."

Alan muttered under his breath, "Jesus Christ." Hana laid one hand on his arm.

"I'll go help," Alan said, taking a few steps toward the doctor.

"Careful," Blackmore said. "I don't want you to step on the chips." He shone the light around the floor, struggling to find them. "They're so damn small. They're hard to see — and even harder to see in this light."

Alan stood back and watched Blackmore, who was now on his hands and knees. The doctor held the light close to the floor as he combed the area, periodically stopping to double-check a spot.

"Alan," Blackmore said. "Would you get me that device I just had? It has a detection system and I can use it to locate the chips. I'm afraid they're too small to see with the naked eye."

Alan made his way over to the side table and felt around for the device. In the semi-darkness, he could barely distinguish it from the other various shapes. "Got it." He walked back toward the doctor.

"Not too close," the doctor said. "Hand it to me."

Alan passed the device to Blackmore, then backed up and watched. The doctor switched off the flashlight and Alan saw only the glow of a small display moving back and forth.

"Got it," Blackmore said finally. There was a note of triumph in his voice. He flicked on the flashlight, licked the end of his finger, and pressed it on the floor. Bringing up his hand, he shone the light on his fingertip then rubbed it over the edge of one of the dishes. He set the dish aside and went back to scanning the floor.

It took another minute, but Blackmore located the other chip. "I'm always amazed when I drop something how far away it can end up. And always in the most unusual nooks and crannies." He got up. "Alan, take the flashlight and guide me over to that table. This time I don't want to run into something and drop the chips again."

Blackmore settled in front of the glowing computer screen and placed the two dishes off to one side. He pulled the black box forward and opened the lid. Taking a pair of tweezers from a drawer, he extracted the first chip from the dish and placed it in the reader. The doctor turned back to the computer screen and clicked through various menus.

"This is Hana's chip," he said. Numbers, symbols, and graphs filled the screen.

Hana leaned in. "Ooh. Is that my brain?"

"Yes," the doctor said as he studied the readouts, but he offered no further explanation.

Hana whispered in Alan's ear, "Wow. I'm impressed with my head." She put a hand on his left buttock, but he reached around and pushed it away.

"Hmm," the doctor said. He opened the black box, exchanged chips, and studied the new readouts. He sat absorbed in the numbers and charts for what seemed an eternity.

Hana whispered to Alan again, "You don't look any different from me. Just as indecipherable." She touched his buttock again, but just as he was about to swat her hand, she pulled it away.

Jaw clenched, Blackmore shut off the monitor and pushed his chair back.

"What's the matter?" Alan said.

"I think the chip's been damaged, probably from the fall. I'm not sure if it's holding your brain's information."

"What does that mean?"

"If we implanted a faulty chip and attempted to restore your original brain configuration, with its memories and thought patterns, there is an almost one hundred percent probability you would be faulty."

"Faulty?"

Blackmore looked at the two of them. "You could be mentally defective. You could be a vegetable, or something less drastic, as in just plain crazy. Whatever the case, we wouldn't be restoring *you*, we'd restore a *damaged* you."

The three of them were silent. Alan had a growing sense of doom. "We don't have a lot of options, do we, Doctor?"

"No. In less than twelve hours, you won't have any options at all. You will be like this permanently."

"Ah, geez." Alan rubbed the back of his neck.

"As much as I have enjoyed the experiment, Dr. Blackmore," Hana said, "I would like to get back to my usual self."

Alan regarded Blackmore. "I hope you have a Plan B in all of this."

"I would have to rescan both your brains and set up new chips. Those new chips would have to be inserted, and we would have to try to re-create the circumstances that caused this to happen in the first place."

"That sounds like a reasonable course of action." Alan ran one hand through his hair. "Okay, Doctor, where do we go from here?"

"At this point, it's your choice. Yes, there are risks. But it's you who must decide whether we go ahead or not."

Alan nodded to Hana. "What do you think?"

"I don't think we have a choice."

Alan thought a moment. "No, we don't have a choice." He spun back to face Blackmore. "Let's do it."

Chapter 15

"I'll get the scanner warmed up. I want you two to make sure the blinds over the windows are pulled down. There's a chance a passing guard may see the light and wonder what's going on. We don't need anybody coming in here to investigate and interrupting the procedure."

Alan and Hana set about shutting all the blinds as tightly as possible. "Too bad these aren't blackout curtains," Hana said.

They heard a buzzing noise: Blackmore sat at the computer system, bathed in the light of the monitor. Alan figured somebody on the outside could still see the light but hoped the next guards would be too busy smoking their dope to notice.

Blackmore had Hana sit and put on the helmet they had seen the previous day. He opened the reader and inserted a chip, then fiddled with controls and examined readouts, tapping his foot.

Alan frowned. "You store a brain's worth of data on a single chip. How much data is there in a brain, anyway?"

"We've estimated the capacity to be around three petabytes."

"Uh, okay. What's a petabyte?"

"A million gigabytes."

"What?"

"A terabyte is one thousand gigabytes, and a petabyte is one thousand terabytes, so that makes a petabyte one million gigabytes."

Alan scrunched his face in confusion. "But on a chip? Does a chip with that capacity even exist?"

"Nanotechnology has led to developments in materials that can be manipulated at an atomic level. Instead of storage being limited to the magnetism of molecules, the polarity of the atom itself can be modified to mimic the basic binary state of information, the fundamental building block of electronic data. It allows for tremendous miniaturization in storage."

"I'm not sure I understood what you said, but since I'm looking at it, I'll have to assume that it's not an illusion."

Blackmore clicked on a menu option. "Finished. Now let's scan *your* brain, Alan."

Hana removed the helmet. "That's it?"

"No," Blackmore said. "I need to scan Alan and transfer the data from both of you to the chips before we can move on to the next step: insertion." He went about placing a second chip in the reader.

Hana stood up and handed the helmet to Alan. He sat down, but before he could put it on, she took his arm. "This is going to be over shortly, but I'm going to miss it." She let go of him. "I'm going to miss you."

Alan said nothing and put on the helmet as Blackmore started the process.

Hana stood behind the doctor and peered over his shoulder at the console. "I have no idea what all that means."

"The brain is a complex organ," Blackmore said. "We've only scratched the surface in understanding how it works."

"I suppose," Hana said, "but you seem to be at the forefront of the research."

"Yes, I suppose I am."

"Don't be modest, Doctor," Hana said. "Your noninvasive BCI is remarkable in comparison with what's being done elsewhere."

Blackmore whirled around. "You know about brain-computer interfaces?"

"I'm not an expert, but I do read. I like to keep up with developments in the scientific community."

"I'm impressed, Ms. Toussaint. I wouldn't have expected you to be versed in such erudite matters."

"I have a cousin who was involved in a BCI test. He has an artificial arm."

"You're an interesting woman."

"Many people think so."

Alan half smiled, listening to the muffled conversation.

Blackmore and Hana were again scrutinizing the console when Hana cocked her head. "Do you hear something?"

She walked to the door and listened carefully. After a

moment, she hurried back to Blackmore. "Somebody's trying the front door."

"It's locked."

"Would security do that?"

"I'm not sure. More than likely somebody has seen the glow through the blinds."

"What do we do?"

"We need to hide." Blackmore checked the computer. "The scan needs another thirty seconds. The two of you can hide behind the workstation partition."

"What about you?"

"There's a utility closet on the opposite side of the room. I can slip in there." Blackmore peeked at the console. "Twenty seconds."

There was a thump from upstairs. Somebody was in the building. Alan glanced up at the ceiling as Hana watched the screen and held up one hand counting down with her fingers. She could hear footsteps in the main corridor overhead as she motioned to Alan. He stood up and gently put the helmet down, then they scurried behind the partition. Blackmore shut off the monitor, got up, and crossed the room.

The footsteps on the linoleum sounded muted, as if the person was trying to sneak around. The door to the lab opened a crack, and a hand reached in and flicked the light switch. A guard sprang through the door into the brightly lit room and scanned the room with a menacing scowl. He stood there a moment before realizing something was buzzing. He walked across the room to examine the junction box and the various wires running down to the helmet. Touching the helmet, he slowly looked around the room. He turned back to the box and pressed a button marked *Power*. The buzzing noise diminished and there was silence. The guard walked back to the far side of the room. He cast a look around one last time, before turning off the lights and closing the door. His footsteps disappeared back down the hall and the building was quiet once again. After a moment, a door slammed in the distance.

The three stayed in their hiding spots for a good minute before coming back out. Each of them tiptoed into the middle of the room, their head tilted, straining to catch the slightest noise.

"That was close," Hana whispered.

"Yes," Dr. Blackmore whispered back. "By a stroke of luck, we just — and I mean *just* — finished Alan's scan. If it had been interrupted, we would have had to start all over again, and I'm sure that if the guard found the scanner turned on a second time, he would know for sure somebody was in here and conduct a more thorough investigation."

"Let's count our blessings," Hana said.

"What's next, Doctor?" Alan asked.

"I need to set up the chips for implant." Blackmore sat down at the desk and turned the monitor back on. He inserted the first chip in the reader and went through the menu. Hana and Alan fidgeted as they followed his movements.

After a moment, Hana tugged at Alan's arm and pulled him away from Blackmore. "What happens if he fails to get us back in our proper bodies?"

"I've been thinking about that," Alan said. "Neither of us could do the other's job. We don't have the requisite knowledge and experience. People — our colleagues, our friends — would soon know something was amiss. Heck, we could both end up committed to psychiatric institutions."

"What would I do as a man?"

"What would I do as a woman?" Alan shrugged his shoulders. "I suppose, since I still have my knowledge of finance, I could return to the industry. But I would have no relevant diplomas to my name. I could write exams and get a certification, but would be without my MBA. It would make it difficult to get my foot in the door at most firms."

"I wonder how I'd do as a gigolo."

Alan's head jerked as he squinted at her. "Seriously, you'd go back to that?"

"It can be profitable work with the right clientele." She shrugged. "But who am I kidding? I'd miss being a woman."

Alan scrunched up his face in exasperation. "Boy, how would I deal with *this*?"

"Being a woman?"

"Yeah. I'm not equipped for it. You're more open about all this, but me? Being a man is who I *am*. I can't imagine how I'd start over."

They stood together in silence.

"This better work," Alan said.

Blackmore swiveled in his seat. "We're ready. First, I'm going to insert the chips in each of you and activate them. However, I must make the same mistake we originally did; that is, I have to configure the chip to do a data dump to the brain. If this succeeds in recreating the original scenario, the updated snapshots of your brains will be transferred back, effectively restoring you to your own bodies."

"Wait a second," Hana said. "I don't understand something. If *that* brain in *that* body" — she pointed to Alan—"was thinking like me, and then you transferred that thinking process and those memories to this head, and now *this* brain and body is me, once we do the whole thing over again in reverse ... What is me? *Where* is me? Is there really a *me* or am I nothing more than a series of thoughts that can be recorded and transferred?"

Blackmore and Alan both looked at her but said nothing.

"If I can be transferred around," she continued, "could I take this thing, this *me*, and transfer it to a new body when I grow old? Could I live forever? But then again, is the *copy* of me actually *me*?"

Blackmore nodded. "You ask questions that philosophers and science fiction writers have been grappling with for years. I don't think anybody has a definitive answer."

"This is getting heavy," Alan said.

"Sorry," Hana said. "It just sprang into my head."

"I would love to debate these issues and more," Alan said, "but this isn't the best time to be working out the epistemological implications of indeterminacy."

"What?" The doctor stared at Alan.

"Never mind, Doctor. Let's get this show on the road."

Blackmore took out his flashlight and picked up the original device. He put in the first chip and studied the readout. "Hana, have a seat," he said, and put the device flush up against the back of her neck.

Alan suddenly grabbed Blackmore's hand and pulled it away. "Are you sure about the chip, Doc?"

"I double-checked. This is your chip. For sure."

"Okay. I want to err on the side of caution."

Blackmore put the device back against Hana's neck. "Get ready." He pressed a button, and there was a slight noise.

"Ow," she said.

"Hold your hand over the back of your neck." Blackmore put the second chip in the device. "Alan, if you would sit?"

Alan and Hana traded places, and the doctor reinserted Alan's chip.

"Once again, are you positive this is the right chip?" Alan rubbed the back of his neck.

"Yes," Blackmore said. "I verified it, and I'm absolutely certain. Let me show you." He held the device up to the back of Hana's neck and pressed some buttons. "Look." There on the display was the name *Alan Maitland.* "That's your body; that's your chip."

"Thanks, Doctor."

"My research is sound," Blackmore said. "It will open doors. But as with any new undertaking, mistakes are made, and I'm no different from anybody else. I regret what has happened, and I'll do my utmost to ensure that this situation is rectified."

"We appreciate that," Alan said.

Hana nodded.

Dr. Blackmore readied the device. "Which one of you wants to go first?"

"Ladies first," Alan said.

Blackmore turned to Alan.

"No, I meant Hana," Alan said.

"Oh. I'm not sure I'm going to get used to that."

"Imagine how *we* feel," Alan said.

Blackmore pulled out a chair. "Hana, would you sit down?"

"What's going to happen?" she asked.

"I'm not sure," Blackmore said. "I guess the same thing as before."

"Wait." Alan creased his brow. "If you put the implants in during the day, why did the switch not occur until hours later?"

"I looked into that. The configuration had been set to turn on the data dump at a specific time. This time, however, I'm doing things manually and have adjusted the setting to ensure that everything happens as soon as I throw the switch."

Hana bit her lip. "I guess we don't really know whether this will work."

"No."

"We don't know what will happen."

"No."

"I have a sense of the risk involved now," Hana said. "I feel like a bolt of lightning is going to come out of the sky and strike me dead."

Alan took her hand. "I'm right here."

She looked up at him. "Thanks."

Alan hesitated before leaning over and kissing her on the lips. "I want to keep seeing you."

"What?"

He cupped one side of her head and kissed her deeply for a prolonged moment. "I want this to work. I want to keep seeing you." He stood and released her hand. "Let's go, Doc."

"Okay." Blackmore glanced at Hana then at the device. He pushed a button.

She sat staring straight ahead. Alan watched her as Blackmore inspected the mechanism.

"What happened?" Alan scrunched up his face, perplexed.

Blackmore tinkered with the controls. "I don't know."

"Hana, are you all right?" Alan leaned over to look at her, but she continued to stare off into the distance. "Hana?" He waved his hand in front of Hana's face. She didn't move. She didn't blink. "Doctor, something isn't right!"

Just then, she let out a low groan and her eyes rolled back in her head, her body going limp. Alan tried to keep her in the chair but her weight, the weight of *his* body, caught him off guard and all he could do was control her fall onto the floor. "Jesus! Doctor!"

Blackmore set down the device and rushed over. He pulled back an eyelid and put two fingers to Hana's throat. "I think her heart has stopped."

"What?"

"Do you know CPR?"

"I'm on it."

"I'm going to get an emergency defibrillator. Get started and keep going until I come back."

Alan moved Hana onto her back and began doing CPR cycles: thirty chest compressions followed by two breaths. He could hear Blackmore running down the hall and heading upstairs. He leaned over the body and pushed down, counting. "Don't you dare die on me," he said under his breath, his own heart pounding.

Blackmore burst back into the room with a small kit. Alan continued compressions while Blackmore grabbed hold of Hana's shirt and yanked. Buttons jingled onto the floor. Blackmore moved like a madman, trying to work fast but carefully. He opened the kit, took out the electrode pads, peeled off the backing, and stuck them to either side of her chest.

The doctor turned on the unit, seized the electrode wires, and plugged them into the machine. "Get ready." Blackmore hit the button marked *Analyze*. A synthesized voice said, "Analyzing rhythm. Everyone stand clear." There was a delay of about five seconds then the voice said, "Shock advised. Charging. Everyone stand clear." There was another pause of about two seconds before a buzzer sounded. The voice continued: "Everyone stand clear. Push the shock button."

Alan moved back as Blackmore pressed the button and Hana's body jerked. The synthesized voice said, "Shock delivered. Begin five cycles of CPR."

Alan wiped his sweaty palms against his skirt and started again. He kept going when the voice said, "One minute of CPR remaining." He continued until he heard, "Analyzing rhythm. Everyone stand clear." He stopped and waited. Alan looked down at Hana, filled with a sense of helplessness. The machine spoke again, "Continue CPR."

As Alan made to do so, Hana gasped. The doctor put one hand to her chest and with the other felt her neck. "She has a pulse — she's breathing," he said.

"Hana?" Alan stared at her face. "Hana?"

Blackmore leaned over and pulled back an eyelid, shining his flashlight into the eye. "She appears to be unconscious." He leaned back and rubbed his forehead.

"What do you think is wrong?" Alan kept staring at her.

"I'm at a complete loss. I've never done this before and have nothing to compare with. What's right? What's wrong? I haven't got a clue."

"We have to do something, Doctor."

Blackmore shook his head. "I don't know what else to try. We have the heart going. The body is breathing. But why is the brain not functioning? Why is the patient unconscious? It's anybody's guess."

Alan wrung his hands. "How do you know the brain isn't functioning? Can you check it? Would that implant tell you something?"

Blackmore furrowed his brow. "Maybe." He got up and fetched the device. "I'm getting a signal from the chip."

"Can you tell anything? Can you detect brain activity?"

"There seems to be something going on, but I don't know what. Even if I see something, I can't tell whose brain activity it is: yours or Hana's. Until the patient regains consciousness, we have no way of knowing what's happened with this reboot."

Alan stood and paced the room. "Jesus, Doctor. What should we do next? If there is nothing you can do, should we consider bringing somebody else in on this?"

"Bring somebody in on this? What do you mean?"

Alan stopped. "I'm suggesting we phone for an ambulance. I'm at a loss what else to do."

"I see your point."

"Of course, I'm sure no hospital would be equipped to handle this condition. If anybody found out the reason this person was like this, there'd be a million questions."

Blackmore nodded. "I hate to think about that."

"Run over everything with me again and make sure you didn't miss anything."

"Well, I recorded a snapshot of your brains. I transferred the data to separate chips. I inserted the chips and confirmed they were the right chips for each body. I set up both send and receive functions on the chip in Hana's body, then turned it on."

"Seems simple enough, Doctor."

Blackmore nodded. "But let's not overlook the fact that the brain is a complex organ. One wrong move, and then what? The whole thing falls over like a house of cards."

Alan pulled out his smartphone and punched the keys. "I'm calling 9-1-1."

Chapter 16

Alan and Dr. Blackmore stood outside behind Building 42, now lit by the flashing lights of an ambulance. The paramedics were inside, loading Hana onto a gurney. Dr. Blackmore had phoned campus security and four guards had responded, curious as to what had taken place. Fortunately, they were all from the night shift and seemed ignorant of the lab's closure. Nobody questioned the doctor's presence on campus.

"Until I know what's going on, I wouldn't want to activate your chip." Blackmore said as they watched Hana being wheeled into the ambulance. "I think it's too dangerous."

"You realize, Doctor, that we're backed into a corner on this," Alan said.

Blackmore remained silent.

"I've lost my identity. I'm no longer Alan with my condo, with my job, with my life; I'm somebody else. I have the knowledge of Alan Maitland but I'm not Alan Maitland. I have my credit cards, my keys, my access codes, even the PIN for my bank account. I've been able to fake it, but only because I've had Hana's help in dealing with people face to face. Thank God for email! Sooner or later, though, I need to show up for work on my own, and when I do, the jig will be up. I can't continue to get away with this deception." Alan rubbed his temple. "But on top of that, as if that wasn't disorientating enough, I'm no longer the same gender. Talk about throwing me for a loop! How does a thirty-eight-year-old man transition into being a woman? I no longer have any idea of which way is up. Put this all together, and I'm no longer living the dream, I'm in the middle of a nightmare: one protracted hallucination."

One of the paramedics jogged over to Alan. "Excuse me, ma'am. You want to ride along?"

"Yes, of course. Where are we going?"

"We're going to head to the Gerard Medical Center."

Alan motioned to Blackmore. "I'll keep you updated."

"I'm going to go back home," Blackmore said, "and check

my original research to see if I can come up with anything." He walked off.

Alan followed the paramedic and climbed into the back of the ambulance. He sat down and looked at Hana, thoughts tumbling through his brain. If the procedure didn't work, if Hana didn't pull through, Alan Maitland ceased to exist. Alan was dead, gone, history. Yet here was Alan Maitland. Alan continued to live, to breathe, to think, to exist. There was this short distance between Hana and himself, between his body and his life and his mind, but it might as well have been between him and another universe. Even though Alan Maitland was right in front of him, he couldn't get back. He was trapped. Alan felt as though he stood at the window looking in on his life but was no longer able to enter. *What am I going to do?*

The ambulance swayed as it navigated through traffic, heading north on First Avenue. Alan remained lost in thought. His mind reeled at the idea of giving up his dream job, his luxurious condo, and what had seemed to be a promising life. He'd have to start all over again. He shook his head. *This can't be happening.* Tears welled in his eyes.

He remembered his childhood. Every summer, his dad rented a cottage for a few weeks and the entire family would live at the beach. It was a fun time and a complete change from life in the suburbs. However, at the end of the vacation, his parents would pack up the car and they would all go back to their regular lives. Alan remembered looking out the back window of the car as the cottage and the beach receded in the distance. The memory of his time there would grow fainter as his attention became more and more focused on going home, getting back to school, and doing what a young boy does in a suburban home.

He now had that same feeling. He was watching the life of Alan Maitland disappear in the distance. It was getting fainter, he was moving on to something else, although he wasn't sure what.

And what about Hana? This woman's life would end right

here, right now. He'd have a chance to carry on, but she wouldn't. Hana had become so important to him during this ordeal; how would he carry on without her?

The ambulance pulled into the emergency entrance of the medical center. The two paramedics hopped out and came around the back. One held out a hand to Alan. "Ma'am."

He took the paramedic's hand and stepped down from the back. *How odd*, he thought as he repeated to himself the word *ma'am*.

He followed the paramedics into the hospital with his wallet, identification, and the company benefits-plan card. He had all the knowledge necessary to make everyone believe that the person lying on the gurney was, in fact, Alan Maitland. There was nobody better than Alan Maitland to fake being Alan Maitland. But that was only as long as Hana remained unconscious. If she woke up, people would ask questions, and eventually, anybody who knew him would definitely know something was wrong.

When asked what his relationship was to the patient, Alan answered that he was the patient's wife. He remembered people joking about relationships labeled as *complicated* but thought there was no better definition of his position right now. However, for access to Hana, it would be far simpler if he fooled the hospital into believing he was the next of kin. He didn't like the idea of finding himself locked out of his own life. Alan almost chuckled when he visualized somebody telling him he wasn't allowed to see himself. There was a comedic side to this, he had to admit.

The mention of cardiac arrest had ER nurses rushing to check on Hana, and Alan found himself caught up in a flurry of activity. It would seem that Code Blue mobilized the forces of ER faster than any other health issue. Strangely, they found nothing wrong with the heart at all and the overall condition of the patient perplexed them. Other than being unconscious, Hana appeared to be healthy. Later, an ER doctor did an EEG and determined that the brain showed normal signs of activity. Why the patient was unconscious, he couldn't say. Further tests would be necessary, but they couldn't be carried out until a specialist did an assessment. The doctor informed Alan that such a thing would not happen at night and would have to wait until the following day.

Alan sat beside the bed and tried to occupy himself by perusing his smartphone. No calls, no email, no texts. The device turned out to be of limited use for dealing with his anxiety and boredom. He flipped through a magazine that had been lying on a side table but kept glancing at his phone, even though it had not rung. What was Blackmore doing? There was no change in Hana, so Alan wandered off to the cafeteria to get himself a coffee and something to eat.

As he walked down the hall, he saw a sign for the washroom. He pushed a door open but looked a second time at the symbol on the door and the word underneath: *Men.* He let the door close and walked to the next one, which read *Women.* He had heard stories about people who traveled to England and made the switch from driving on the right to driving on the left so seamlessly, it was almost natural. Was he ever going to remember that he was a woman? Was he truly going to make the switch?

A sign in front of the cafeteria indicated that it was open twenty-four hours. He found the place almost empty. A lone cafeteria employee sat at the cash register, playing with an electronic device. Alan picked up a tray and slid it down the line. Since there was no cook on duty, the menu was limited to sandwiches or plates that could put in a microwave. He picked out a chicken salad sandwich and a yogurt with granola. Just before he reached the cashier, he poured himself a cup of coffee.

Having paid, Alan took his tray and wandered into the seating area, choosing a place off to one side. He peeked at his phone again, but there were still no messages. As he sat down, he noticed Jack sitting at another table. He briefly wondered why his coworker would be at the hospital before turning his attention to his food. He unwrapped the sandwich and was about to take a bite when a voice said, "May I join you?"

He looked up to see Jack standing before him, holding a tray. He pointed to the seat across from him. "By all means."

"Thank you." Jack set his tray down, pulling out the chair. "Hana, isn't it?"

"Yes."

"I didn't expect to see anybody here that I know."

"I'm not sure hospitals are the 'in' place to hang out."

Jack sipped his coffee. "What brings you here at such an ungodly hour?"

Alan hesitated. Honesty may be the best policy, but that didn't seem like a good idea at the moment. "I'm here visiting a friend."

"At this hour, I would presume something dramatic."

"Unexpected, but so far unknown. Hopefully, some tests will solve the mystery." He continued eating his sandwich. "But what about you? Being here at this hour can't be good."

"No, unfortunately. My mother had a heart attack, and the expectation at the moment is that she won't last the night."

"I'm sorry."

Jack shrugged. "It's to be expected."

Alan examined his plate and tried to decide which of the two pickles to eat first. He picked up one and glanced at Jack. There was a tear welling in his eye, and as Alan watched, it spilled over and streamed down his cheek. Jack took out a tissue and dabbed at his face.

"Are you all right?" Alan put his food down.

"Yes," Jack said, but choked up.

Alan reached across the table and laid his hand on top of Jack's. "I'm sorry. It can be hard."

Jack said nothing, but cast his eyes downward. He looked like he was struggling with his emotions. After a moment, he let out a sob and his body shook. He turned his hand over and gripped Alan's. "I'm sorry. I ... I'm going to miss her." Jack sniffed a couple of times then half smiled. "I apologize. That must be a little unsightly." He looked down at his hand holding Alan's, and quickly let go. "Pardon me."

"Not at all. It's a tough situation."

They talked for a while about hospitals, the agony of waiting, and how the night crew seemed to be so different from those who worked during the day.

"I should be getting back up," Jack said eventually.

"I should do likewise."

"You seem like a nice lady."

"Thank you." Alan smiled.

"I hope things work out between you and Alan. He's a good guy."

"Good luck with your mother."

Jack picked up his tray. "Thanks." He walked over to a wheeled cart and slid the tray into a slot. He paused at the exit and waved one last time.

Alan mulled over that last remark: *I hope things work out between you and Alan.* It was odd, but he had grown more than fond of Hana over the past couple of days. He thought about everything that had happened to the two of them, a lifetime of experiences in under forty-eight hours. He wanted this to continue. Even if Dr. Blackmore couldn't restore them to their original bodies, Alan realized, he wanted more than ever to be with Hana. At the moment, he felt comfortable with her, and it seemed he could be open with her about anything. They had been through so much together. They hadn't just shared each other's moments — they had actually *lived* each other's moments. They had walked a mile in each other's shoes and then some. After this, how could anybody else compete? He had experienced a depth of connection with Hana that he had never had with anyone else before in his life. All of his relationships had been unique, but this was different — *really* different. People joked about getting inside somebody's head. *If they only knew!*

Alan finished his late-night meal and wandered back to Hana's room. The lights were dimmed, and she hadn't moved. The various readouts showed the heart was working fine and breathing was normal. She appeared to be asleep. There didn't seem to be anything else to do but wait. *Wait for what?* For Hana to wake up? For Blackmore to call? Alan was itching to do something, but felt helpless because there seemed to be nothing he *could* do.

He sat down and looked around. Picking up the magazine, he glanced at the cover and tossed it back on the side table. He sighed and leaned back in his chair. *What to do?* He shut his eyes.

Chapter 17

Alan stirred. He glanced at a wall clock and saw that it was four-thirty a.m. He yawned and stretched his arms as his phone vibrated in his lap. He went into the hall and answered it. "Hello?"

"Alan? This is Dr. Blackmore."

"Have you found anything?"

"I'm not one hundred percent certain, but yes. I believe I found a glitch in the chip configuration that may have led to the phenomenon we witnessed tonight."

"Meaning?"

"When a data transfer takes place, information is buffered in a temporary holding area. When the transfer is complete, the data itself is verified with a checksum process to ensure accuracy. If it's not accurate, the transfer can be carried out a second time. But if the data does prove to be accurate, the system is suspended, and the data is moved from the buffer into live memory. Once that step is complete, the suspension is terminated and the system returns to its operational state. I believe that your chip is in a state of suspension and so has suspended consciousness. The brain is fully operational and doing its work, including all autonomic functions, but Hana — I mean *you* — is essentially asleep."

Alan took the phone away from his ear and stared at it, uncomprehending. He put it back and said, "Okay, Doctor. I'll take your word for it. I trust you've come up with a way of getting the chip out of suspension."

"Yes. However, it would seem that phoning for an ambulance may not have been the right thing to do in the long run."

"You mean ...?"

"The equipment I need is back at the lab."

Alan paced the width of the hall. "Dr. Blackmore, I'm not sure the staff is going to let me wheel an unconscious man out of the hospital."

"I know. We have to sneak Hana out."

"This sounds like a violation of hospital regulations."

"I'm sure it is, but we can't wait. Don't forget that starting this morning at nine the chancellor is going to have my lab taken apart, which means I'll no longer have access to the necessary equipment. We need to do this *now*."

"Suggestions about transportation?"

"I'm parked behind the hospital. I'm coming in now. Where are you?"

Alan looked at the sign on the wall outside Hana's room. "Medical ICU, monitoring room two."

"Got it." Blackmore hung up.

Alan walked back into the room and glanced at Hana, reflecting on the fact that she was a six-foot man weighing one hundred and eighty pounds. This wasn't going to be easy. What else could they do? *Use a wheelchair? Or a gurney?* He looked around. Where was he going to get either?

He walked down the middle of the room and looked at each of the other five patients. All were asleep, their various monitors displaying the status of their health. At the end of the row, he noticed a wheelchair. The man lying on the bed had a cast on one foot. Alan scanned the area for anybody watching, then pulled the chair into the middle of the room. He grabbed the handles and pushed it down to Hana's bed. He studied Hana and the chair. There was no way he could get her safely out of the bed and into the wheelchair. He was going to need the doctor's help.

Blackmore walked in and looked at the wheelchair. "We really need a gurney."

"I don't see one."

"This is going to be tough. Not impossible, but tough."

"You're a doctor. Why can't you sign him out?"

"It's five o'clock in the morning. Nobody's going to release an unconscious man into my care at this hour without asking a lot of questions. We'd be held up for hours with bureaucratic red tape."

Alan pointed to a sensor clip attached to Hana's left index finger. "What about this? I assume removing it will set off an alarm at the nurses' station."

Blackmore pulled back the curtain to the next bed. "I know ICU has suffered from alarm fatigue, and they've added a signal delay to stop false positives." He undid the clip from Hana's finger and attached it to his own. "Minor variances in monitoring are recorded but don't trigger an alarm." He moved to the next bed and transferred the clip to a finger of the neighboring patient.

The doctor studied Hana and the wheelchair once more. "Let's get him dressed. I mean, her."

Alan found Hana's clothes in a small closet by the bed. The two of them struggled with her limp body as they got her out of the hospital gown and back into the suit.

"Let's do this together." Blackmore picked up Hana's legs and moved them over the side of the bed. "Lock it."

Alan moved the chair into position and pulled the brake handle to lock the wheels.

"I'm going to grab her around the chest, lift, and turn her," the doctor said. "You assist me in getting her into a seated position."

"She's one eighty."

"I noticed. I hope I don't pull a muscle or slip a disc."

Blackmore grabbed Hana and grunted as he lifted her from the bed. "Geez, this dead weight is a lot." Eventually, they got the unconscious body seated.

"She's going to keep flopping forward," Alan said, scanning the room for ideas. "Hold her." He saw a bathrobe hanging on a hook and pulled out the tie. He looped it diagonally around Hana's chest then fished it around the back of the chair and tied it in a knot. "It isn't much, but it'll help. We're going to have to push with one hand and keep another on her shoulder."

"One more thing," Blackmore said. He took some pillows and stuffed the sheets so it looked like a body was still in the bed. "It isn't much, but it'll have to do."

The doctor peeked out into the hall. "When I arrived, nobody was at the nurses' station but now there is. I'm certain a wheelchair's going to pique her curiosity. We need a diversion."

"Get Hana out in the hall as close as possible to the station," Alan said. "I'm going to see if I can get the nurse to turn away."

He walked down to the station. A nurse sat behind the counter looking at charts and consulting a computer screen.

"Sorry to trouble you," Alan said.

"Yes?"

"I'm sitting with my husband, and I seem to have run into a problem."

The nurse looked up from her work. "What sort of problem?"

"I've ..." He lowered his eyes. "I've run out of tampons."

The nurse nodded. "I may be able to help you out." She got up from the desk and went into a back office. Alan could see her through the window, examining the contents of a large purse. He heard something behind him and turned to see Blackmore going past the station and down the main corridor to the door leading out of ICU.

The nurse came back and handed Alan a packaged tube. "This should tide you over. The pharmacy on the main floor opens at eight."

"Thank you. You've been very kind." He walked to where Blackmore stood and held the door open. The doctor pushed Hana through, and he followed quickly after.

"We have to turn right and head to the back of the building," Blackmore said.

Looking around, they discovered they were alone. Blackmore pushed Hana down the hall while Alan kept a lookout, not knowing what they would do if anybody challenged them. When they reached the back exit, the doctor was about to head down the ramp when he pointed to two orderlies standing outside smoking. "We don't need anybody asking us any questions."

Alan thought a moment and said, "Leave this to me." He unbuttoned the top two buttons of his blouse and parted the placket. He looked down at his chest, fiddled with the material, then cupped his breasts and lifted.

"What are you doing?" Blackmore said.

"You'll see," Alan said. "Get ready to go."

Alan moved to the doors outside of which the employees were standing, then began his exaggerated sexy walk. He sashayed out and stood close to the men. The first one stared and poked his friend. The second man turned around.

"Hello," one of the men said.

Alan smiled warmly at him. "Good morning. I don't suppose a girl could bum a cigarette?"

The man smiled back. "I think I could help you out."

"Much obliged." Alan positioned himself so that both men had to turn to him with their backs to the wheelchair ramp. The first orderly offered his open pack of cigarettes.

Alan took one and said, "Thanks." The man held out a lighter, and Alan put the cigarette to his lips and leaned over. He took a puff but was careful not to inhale, not wanting to cough and look like an amateur. "Ah, that tastes good," he said, smiling at both men. He ran his fingertips down along the edge of his placket and over the exposed curve of his breast. Neither man bothered to look at Blackmore pushing the unconscious Hana down the ramp to his car.

Alan talked with the men as he covertly observed Blackmore get Hana into the car and the chair into the trunk. Blackmore waved at him and he excused himself. "I see my ride is here. Thanks for the cigarette!"

On their way back to the lab, Alan twisted to look at Hana in the back seat; her head had flopped forward on her chest. "I hope this works."

"I wanted to talk to you about the details."

"Do I hear an 'uh-oh' coming up, Doctor?"

"I scanned your brains around ten-thirty p.m. What's on the chips is a record from that precise moment. Everything that has happened afterward — using the defibrillator, going to the hospital, what we're doing now — is not on those chips. If the restoration works correctly, you will remember events only up to ten-thirty last night, nothing afterward."

Alan scratched his head.

"That part of it is a certainty," the doctor said. "It's logical. But — and this is the big but — I have no idea if *any* of the new memories will be properly restored. Each of your brains could go back to their state forty-eight hours ago, before all this first happened. In other words, there is a chance neither of you would have the slightest recollection of anything that has taken place in the past two days."

Alan remained silent. He stared out the window as the nighttime street went by.

"Did you understand that?" Blackmore said.

"Yes." Alan sighed. "I can't say I'm all that pleased with such a prospect."

"Would this be comparable to having a nightmare, then waking up and not being able to remember a thing?"

"I suppose. But, Doctor, I *want* to remember all this. It may have been a nightmare, as you put it, but it's also been an extraordinary experience."

"I can't make any guarantees."

Arriving at the university, Blackmore parked in a rear lot close to the building. As Alan helped him get Hana into the wheelchair, a car pulled to a stop in front of their vehicle and a blinding white light shone upon them. "Doctor Blackmore, you're under arrest."

They each held up a hand over their eyes, and Alan could see the flashing lights of a campus police car. Doors opened and two security guards came out of the shadows. The first guard pulled out a pair of handcuffs as he walked up to Blackmore. "If you don't mind, Doctor." He turned Blackmore around and handcuffed him. "You have the right to remain silent. Anything you say can and will be used against you in a court of law. You have the right to an attorney. If you cannot afford an attorney, one will be provided for you. Do you understand your rights?"

Blackmore squinted in the glare of the light. "I don't understand. What's going on? I'm not a criminal."

"Trespassing, Dr. Blackmore," the guard said. "The night watch informed the chancellor of your earlier visit and ordered you brought in if you showed up again on campus."

"But you can't stop me now," Blackmore said. "I have to complete the procedure. This man's life depends on it."

"There's a second charge of assault with intent."

"What?"

"Whatever you were doing last night resulted in an ambulance being called. The chancellor said you had no right to enter the building, never mind perform a procedure."

"But this is all a mistake!"

The second guard looked at Alan. "Are you Hana Toussaint?"

"Yes." Alan held one hand over his eyes, trying to see through the blinding light.

"I'm afraid I have to arrest you too, but I'll forgo the cuffs."

"What? What did I do?" There was a tightness in Alan's chest.

"I've been told you're a possible accomplice."

"You're kidding me!"

The guard shrugged. "I'm sorry. I don't have all the details. This is something the lawyers will have to work out."

"Lawyers? This is crazy!"

The first guard looked down at Hana. "Is this man in need of medical attention?"

"No," Blackmore said. "I need to get him to the lab."

"He's unconscious. Does he need an ambulance?"

"No. I'm a doctor." Blackmore ran a hand over his brow. "Please, I just need to him get to the lab."

"Hold on a sec." The guard pulled out a cellphone and dialed. "Chancellor Cole, we have Dr. Blackmore in custody. He parked in back lot five and was about to enter the lab." He paused. "Yes, sir, he's got the man. He claims he's okay." He listened closely. "What would you like to do?"

The guard listened again then said, "Yes, sir." He put the phone back in a pocket before saying, "Chancellor Cole has instructed us to take you to the lab. He'll meet us there in forty-five minutes."

Blackmore and Alan sat nervously in the reception area with the unconscious Hana. The guard had agreed to take the cuffs off the doctor, believing he didn't present a flight risk. A wall clock showed seven a.m. when the main door of Building 42 opened and in walked a silver-haired, distinguished gentleman followed by a military man dressed in uniform.

The doctor whispered to Alan, "Chancellor Kurt Cole."

"You've gone too far, Julian," Cole said. "You sent a man to the hospital. You've exposed the university to a lawsuit. And you've trespassed on university property: you disobeyed my orders."

"Now listen, Kurt—"

"Kurt? Kurt? *Chancellor* Cole to you. You're in big trouble."

"Ahem."

Everyone turned to look at the man in uniform standing to one side.

"This is Major James Channon of the United States Air Force. He's an advisor to the Board of Regents."

Major Channon walked over to Hana.

"Do you see what he's done, Major?" Cole gestured to the wheelchair.

Channon leaned down to look at Hana. "What's the matter with him?"

"He's unconscious," Blackmore said.

"Is he okay?"

The doctor shrugged. "He'd be up and about if we hadn't been stopped."

Channon looked at Blackmore. "Stopped from what?"

"I need to carry out a procedure to bring Mr. Maitland around."

The Chancellor pointed at Hana. "See? See? This is what got us into this mess! Julian, you can't go around trying these cockamamie procedures on people. I told you it was ineffective."

"Just the opposite, Kurt. I've made a remarkable

discovery," Blackmore said confidently.

"What are you babbling about?"

"I've managed to switch the minds of these two people."

There was a long silence as everyone looked at each other.

"What?" Cole threw up his hands. "You've got to be kidding me! This is crap. This is the delusional raving of a lunatic. You're desperate to hold on to your funding, and you'll make up any farfetched story to justify it."

"It's true. Just ask Alan." Blackmore pointed and everyone turned to Alan.

Alan looked at the Major. "Hello, Jimmy."

The Major raised an eyebrow. "Do I know you?"

"James Channon and Alan Maitland are friends," Alan said.

"It's a parlor trick," Cole insisted. "She could have been coached."

Channon studied Alan. "It's possible, but I have no idea why Alan would participate in such a scheme."

"Do you know this man?" Cole pointed at Hana.

"Yes. That's why I asked to be here. I recognized the name in the incident report."

"With all due respect, Major," Cole said, "this is the wrong way of going about it. We've had far more success with the traditional approaches to BCI than Blackmore's craziness. He's not only barking up the wrong tree, he's wasting grant money that could be better spent elsewhere."

Channon looked at Hana then looked back at Alan. "How could you conclusively prove right here, right now, that anything Professor Blackmore just said is true?"

"May we speak in private?" Alan gestured to the other side of the room. The major nodded his head and the two of them walked to the far corner of the room. Alan leaned closer and whispered. The Major's eyes widened. He took a step back and stared at Alan.

"Chancellor Cole." Channon walked back to the waiting group. "I think Professor Blackmore deserves the opportunity to prove himself."

"What?" Cole said. "Major, you're kidding? This is

poppycock."

"No; I would like to hear the professor out. It won't take long, and if the professor fails to prove his point, we can continue with your course of action."

"This is nonsense. Pure nonsense."

***

Blackmore pushed the wheelchair carrying Hana toward the lab. Cole and Channon followed. The doctor leaned over to whisper to Alan. "What did you say to Major Channon to convince him you were really you?"

"Jimmy and I met at summer camp when we were in our early teens. We were going through puberty and discovering our sexuality. The two of us spent some time exploring our newfound urges together."

The doctor stared ahead as he pushed the wheelchair. Suddenly, his eyes widened, and he said, "Oh."

"It was a long time ago — the curiosity of youth. It was a moment in time, never to be repeated, and certainly never to be divulged. Jimmy has been happily married now for twenty years and has two kids."

In the lab, Blackmore turned on the computer system. He pointed to one side. "Kurt, Major Channon, stand over there, please. Do not interfere. This is a delicate procedure." He moved Hana and set about getting the helmet on her head. "I'll need ten minutes to verify the chip configuration."

Alan wandered out into the hall, holding his phone. He paced nervously then stopped. He checked the phone for available data storage and went through the menu to set up a video recording. He held the phone in front of him and pressed *Record*.

"Hello, Alan, this is Alan. Yes, the woman you're looking at is actually you. I'm going to tell you a story, a story so incredible you aren't going to believe it. However, there's a Dr. Blackmore who can confirm everything I'm about to tell you." He glanced at the phone. "There's a chance you may not

148

remember anything that has taken place in the past forty-eight hours. I'm recording this in the hope that it will remind you of the most extraordinary experience you've ever had."

Alan went on to explain about the chips, the snapshot of the brains, and the transfer of data — all with the realization that anyone seeing this video would think he had lost his mind. He hit the pause button. *What else is there to say, to explain?* The more he thought about it, the more absurd the situation seemed. The last two days had been way too bizarre, too crazy. If he didn't remember anything, there was no way he was going to give any credence to this video. When he watched it, he would simply think he was listening to the ramblings of a crazed woman.

Alan again pressed *Record* and finished a few thoughts. He now believed this was stupid, but he shrugged. *What the heck — it's worth a shot.*

He went back into the room.

"I'm ready," Blackmore said. He clicked through several menus on the system monitor then glanced at Alan. "This is it. Keep your fingers crossed." He selected the final option and everyone stared at Hana.

"I don't see any reaction, Doctor." Alan kept staring at Hana as he moved his head to a different angle.

"Hmm, so it seems. I—"

Hana's eyes blinked.

"Look, Doctor!"

Hana blinked again. Her gaze moved between the doctor and Alan. "Where am I?"

"What's your name?" Blackmore said.

"What?"

"What is your name?"

"My name?" Hana frowned. "What's the matter? Did something happen to me?"

"What's your name?"

"Alan Maitland."

Blackmore broke into a grin. "Do you know where we are?"

The restored Alan turned his head, surveying the room. "I have no idea what this place is. The last thing I remember was going to sleep in my condo."

The Alan in Hana's body leaned closer. "Who am I?"

Alan, the man, studied the woman's face. "I don't recognize you. Should I?"

Blackmore sighed. "I warned you about this in the car. The new memories haven't been restored. What originally happened to the two of you must have been a fluke. It looks like his memory has gone back to what it was before the initial incident." He shook his head. "There's so much I still don't know. I wish I had more time, more staff, more funding ... The answer is out there. I just have to persist in looking for it."

He removed the helmet, and the restored Alan stood up. "How do you feel?" Blackmore asked.

Alan said, "Okay, I guess. I feel as though I should know something, but I can't remember what."

The Alan in Hana's body narrowed his eyes. "You have no idea who I am?"

"No."

"Damn."

The restored Alan glanced around. He stared at the major. "Jimmy? James Channon?"

"Yes," Channon said.

"What are *you* doing here?"

"We'll talk later."

Blackmore adjusted the chip device. "Let's do *you* now, Alan."

The Alan in Hana's body said "Okay" at the same time the restored Alan said "What?"

The doctor pointed to Hana's body. "I mean him. I mean *her.* Whatever!"

Alan sat down and stared at the helmet. He took a deep breath and put it on. Blackmore went through the same procedure then stared at the body sitting in the chair. "What is your name?"

The woman blinked at the doctor. "I'm Hana Toussaint.

And you are?"

Blackmore grinned. "Ah, success!"

"Sorry? I don't understand. Where am I? Who are you?" She looked around the lab. "How did I get here?"

Alan regarded the woman in the chair. "It would seem, Ms. Toussaint, that you and I share the fate of being thrust into the same unknown set of circumstances." He stuck out a hand. "Alan Maitland."

"In any other situation, charmed." She took his hand and raised her eyebrows at Blackmore. "Who are you? What's going on?"

"Long story." Blackmore sighed. "But first, let's get those chips out of you."

Chapter 18

Alan stood at the balcony railing sipping a Scotch. He was looking down the bustling street when his phone vibrated in his pocket. "Hello?"

"Alan, it's Dr. Blackmore."

"Good evening."

"It's been two weeks now since the restoration. I wanted to get an update. How are you doing?"

"Good. Perfect. My memory has been completely restored: up to, and including, your last scan. I don't understand the delay of twenty-four to forty-eight hours, but they are definitely all back."

"That baffles me. I can only guess it took time for your neurons to process the new memories and make them accessible to your conscious mind — although, I still have no idea how this happened in the first place. I have a lot of research to do."

"I have no doubt that you'll find the answer. I think you've hit on something that certainly opens the door to a brand-new way of conducting BCI."

"Thank you. It's unfortunate not everyone sees my work that way."

Alan smiled. "How is the good chancellor?"

"The major put in a word for me with the Board of Regents. The military has suddenly become very interested in my work, and increased my funding. The chancellor has been given strict orders not to interfere."

"I'm not surprised. I hope you've been lenient with Kyle."

"I admit, I was angry over his screw-up, but I owe this turn of fortune to his mistake. There've been a number of discoveries that occurred because of an accident — penicillin, radioactivity, even Coca-Cola." Blackmore paused. "Despite the problems, Alan, I hope you'll consider participating in my program again."

Alan chuckled. "That's kind of you to think of me, Doctor. I'll mull it over carefully, as I'm still trying to sort things out from this time."

"We're all pioneers in science!"

"I suppose, but it might be a bit more of a contribution to research than I'm willing to make at the moment. Next time a donation will suffice."

"Please keep me in mind, Alan. I appreciate your help. Keep in touch. Good night."

"Good night, Doctor." Alan put his phone back in his pocket.

A hand touched his arm and Hana smiled up at him.

"Hello, you," he said. He leaned over and kissed her. "How was your day?"

"Promising. Mr. Smith says he's convinced his wife to come in so they can see me as a couple. I'm sure I can renew their relationship and give the two of them a fresh start. He said they'll be celebrating thirty years of marriage next year, and he'd like to go for another thirty."

"You're the one to help them do it!"

"By the way, would you go to the christening of Marvin's son this coming Saturday?"

"Sure."

"Thanks. I know he'll be pleased." Hana nestled against him. "So, how was your day?"

"I've signed up. My first French class is this Thursday."

"*C'est magnifique.* I know you'll do well. You've got the drive."

"Let's say I'm now well-motivated. Fagler signed the contract, so I'm going to be dealing with the French company on a regular basis."

"I'm always willing to help." She glanced over the railing. "Whatcha doin' out here?"

Alan put an arm around her shoulders. "You know me. I enjoy looking out over the city, watching the people in the street."

"On top of the world."

"Yes, on top of the world." They snuggled close as they gazed over the cityscape.

Alan had eventually found the video he had recorded that night. It didn't quite tell the whole story, and he was thankful his memories had come back or he would never have appreciated what had happened. He still chuckled over the end of the video, when, in the body of Hana, he said, "Yes, Alan, I know it's difficult to believe any of this, but it's all true. The doctor can corroborate some of it, but you'll have to take my word on the rest. Oh, and one more thing. That woman, Hana Toussaint? For God's sake, don't let her get away. She's the one."

Acknowledgements

I thank NaNoWriMo. They inspired me to find the self-discipline to sit at my desk day after day doing something other than looking at cat videos. However, it took a number of people to help me unravel the disjointed, illogical, non sequitur, stream of consciousness crammed full of so many spelling mistakes and grammatical errors, anyone would think I had failed English and failed it miserably. What did I know about writing? The first time somebody told me I had a dangling participle, I checked to see if my fly was open.

Editors, beta readers, and copyediting people have corrected me, counseled me, and sometimes told me *no* in the hope I would end up stringing two words together to make a coherent sentence — or go away. They get the credit for their patience, kindness, and experienced assistance. I get the blame for the results.

Chris Banks (his editing software ProWritingAid)
Joanie Chevalier
Dorothy Davies
Jennifer Dinsmore
Stephanie Fysh
Karine Green
Dave King (and his book, "Self-Editing for Fiction Writers")
Stephen King (his book: On Writing)
Elmore Leonard (10 Rules for Good Writing)
Bobbie Morgan (1964-2015)
Ray Rhamey (and his book "Flogging the Quill")
Una Verdandi
Lila Weekes
D. A. Wolf (and her web site Daily Plate of Crazy)

Beta readers: they are too numerous to mention, but I sincerely thank each and every one of them. They pointed out things I didn't see or couldn't see. I wear glasses, however it turns out I'm myopic literally and literarily.

About the Author
William Quincy Belle is just a guy. Nobody famous; nobody rich; just some guy who likes to periodically add his two cents worth with the hope, accounting for inflation, that $0.02 is not over evaluating his contribution. He claims that at the heart of the writing process is some sort of (psychotic) urge to put it down on paper and likes to recite the following, which so far he hasn't been able to attribute to anyone: "A writer is an egomaniac with low self-esteem." You will find Mr. Belle's unbridled stream of consciousness floating around in cyberspace.

Other books by this author

Life, Love and the Big D
10 Short Stories About How Things Work Out
We're born. We die. We marry. We divorce. Here are ten short stories about how things work out. Sometimes it's good, and sometimes it's bad. However, no matter what the results are, no matter the pain and anguish we all live through or the happiness we find, this is our life. As a wise man once said, "If you hang in there long enough, you'll grow old and die."

Coming November 2016

Why Fi: Vol. 1
5 Short Stories of Speculative Fiction
Science fiction or speculative fiction? Here are short stories speculating about the future when science has figured it all out: outer space, inner space, rocket ships, teleportation, alternate worlds and alternate realities. The future looks interesting, even exciting, but it's not without its dangers.

Coming December 2016

Why Fi: Vol. 2
10 More Short Stories of Speculative Fiction
Further speculation about the future and science.

Connect with William Quincy Belle

Like my book? Tell your friends. Didn't like it? Please don't firebomb my house.

Visit me on my web site:
http://www.williamquincybelle.com

Friend me on Facebook:
https://www.facebook.com/WilliamQuincyBelle

Follow me on Twitter:
https://twitter.com/wqbelle

Stalk me on Google.
https://www.google.com

www.ingramcontent.com/pod-product-compliance
Lightning Source LLC
Chambersburg PA
CBHW021021120726
47905CB00009B/3117